BOOK TWO

THE CRYSTAL OF LIFE

RAHEEM D. ALLEN

I Am Rick LLC.

LOUISIANA

All rights reserved. Published by I Am Rick LLC.

No part of this book may be reproduced or transmitted in any form

Or by any means, electronic or mechanical, including photocopying, recording, or by

Any information storage and retrieval system, without written

permission from the publisher.

I Am Rick LLC.

raheemdallen@gmail.com

First Paperback Edition: August 2013

The characters and events portrayed in this book are fictitious. Any similarity

To real persons, living or dead, is coincidental and not intended by the author.

Library of Congress Cataloging-in-Publication Data on file.

ISBN – 13: 978-0615899756

ISBN – 10: 0615899757

Printed in the United States of America

To friends, they make the journey more fun.

Also by

Raheem Allen

The I Am Rick Series

I Am Rick: Zane's Destruction

CONTENTS

PROLOGUE - Obituary/1

PROLOGUE

Obituary

The crunching sound of grass beneath my boots told me that it had just finished raining. The condensation in the air made my senses tingle. Even in the light of the moon, the fog from my breathing was visible through my Guardian eyes. There, where I stood I gathered my surroundings. I remembered the last time I was there, an unpleasant experience. I bent down to one knee and I sensed the cold stone laying amongst the grass. I slowly removed my Power Glove and revealed the symbol on the back of my right hand.

I would not call it a tattoo because it is more permanent than that. It is a remembrance of a certain someone I love. It is a symbol of power and friendship.

Friendship.

Power.

I slid my bare hand onto the cold slab that layed in front of me feeling the grooves of the writing engraved onto it. My body came to a stop when the symbol on my hand met with the same complete symbol on the slab.

Fiona….

Using my enhanced vision, I re-read the writing on the slab even though I had it memorized word for word:

FIONA CHAROLETTE VERDETT

May 12, 2052 - March 28, 2068

"A Beloved Lady with a Passion for Trouble."

So many names and memories flooded back into my head all at once. What she fought for. Why she died. The many times we spent together.

And Zane.

My mouth tasted bitter as I remembered the name. He was the one who killed her. He was the one that destroyed the city, not me. He was the reason why I was wanted. Bah, enough. I did not want his presence to infect what I felt for Fiona. Let the dead rest. And good riddance to Zane. But he does not deserve rest, he deserves hell. His face is forever etched into my brain no matter how many times I try to scrub it off.

"Rick, it's time to go," I heard Jay say from the darkness. Jay and the others were waiting on me. I should have never came there, I was not ready. I stood back up and wiped the condensation from my pants. I slipped my Power Glove back on and took one last glance at Fiona's grave. Then as I slowly turned around to face my friends, I felt a slight itch on the symbol on my right hand. I ignored it as I walked away from my beloved…

CHAPTER I

Infamous

"Don't let your emotions speak for you," Dane offered as he patted me on the back. He was right, Dane is usually right. Hm, how can I describe Dane to you? I know it may sound cheesy but Dane was the loveable, big fellah of the group. Kind of self-explanatory, right? Besides me, he was the only black guy in the group and we got along pretty well. I looked back at him and gave him a reassuring smile.

Saturday, July 28th, 2068. New York, New York. My friends and I were in a waiting area just standing around, waiting. All of us, teens, were gonna be on worldwide television in ten minutes. I looked at all of their hardened faces: Jay, Sam, Dane, Lance, Antoine, Brooke, Sabrina, Keith, Arlene and Tensar the Pomega. My friends, my arsenal. I could count on these guys for anything. We all had been through a lot and we already trusted each other dearly. There was just one person missing though…

"Alright guys," I started. "Stay sharp and only say what is needed. Don't try to give out too much information and unless instructed otherwise, I will be doing all the talking." Jay then grunted from the corner he was standing in. "You mad, bro?" I asked quoting some retro comic I had read.

"No, I'm not mad," Jay said sharply. "But what if I want to speak for my own accord and not follow your rules? You know I don't like rules," Then he gave me a quick frown. "Bro."

"Well, then that would probably get us killed," Lance replied before I could open my mouth.

"He's right," I said. "This could either make us or break us with the humans."

"Why does it matter?" Jay spoke up again. "Let's just go home."

"No," I simply said. "We're here now, too late to turn back. Besides, the last time I was on TV I was a mess."

"Hmm, well I think we should somehow hide our weapons to not provoke the humans," Antoine suggested. I glanced around the room and then to everyone's weapons and then down to my own, newly acquired, sword. "He's right," I said. "Everyone give your weapons to Tensar. If anything goes down, we have our Guardian powers under our sleeves. Tensar you stay here. I'm pretty sure the humans don't want you around anyway."

"Gotcha," he said to all of us telepathically. Tensar was my first real friend. Pomegas are friendly, giant, flying creatures with enormous wings. They almost looked like giant colorful bees, but very, very different. When I was little I found him (or he found me) in an area we liked to call The Hideout. I hung out with him and the rest of his creature friends until I went to Baton Rouge's School for the Mind, Body and Soul. That's where I met the rest of my friends and my new life began. As Tensar relieved us of our weapons, a woman called for us over the intercom and told us to go to the backstage. We waved good-bye to the Pomega and headed on our way.

As we walked through the backstage, the workers ushered us into a straight line at a door until they called us. "What are we, four?" Lance asked from the back of the line. I stayed quiet and practiced my facial expressions since I was the first in line. I am the leader of this whole Tinsletown operation. So, I gotta show some leadership. Leaders are supposed to be bold, courageous, good – looking and strong. All of the things that I think I'm not. But there I was.

I pushed open the door once the head worker said it was okay and I walked out onto the little panel they set up for us. I sat down in one of the middle chairs and Jay took the other. The rest filed in randomly behind us. The reporters, police officers, SWAT, camera operators and other observers were all staring at us like we were a dance group from the 1960's. I didn't blame them though. We all wore our black Power Gloves with our elements symbols on them, black boots and cargo pants with our magical long sleeved black shirts that made us look like cosplayers.

Cameras flashed in my eyes and I surveyed the surroundings. They were all frightened! Ha, change of plans. "You can begin asking questions," someone said from behind us. Quickly, hands flew up from everywhere in the crowd. "You first," Jay whispered to me and he gave a faint laugh as he went back into position.

"Uhh," I said as I pointed at a guy in the back. "You with the brown jacket!"

Everyone in the crowd became silent. All attention was on him now. "Who or what are you people?" he asked with a little flair in voice. "Why are you here?" There was obvious agreement from the crowd.

"We like to call ourselves Guardians," I started. "We protect the Earth."

"Protect Earth?" someone asked from the back. "You people destroyed that city in Louisiana in a day!" There was a giant roar of "Yeah!" from the supporters.

"What you saw was a very disturbed mind on a rampage," I stated. "The rest of us aren't like that. We aren't here to hurt you."

"Oh really?" questioned a gruff voice to the left of me. Brooke, who was on the other side of me, grabbed my hand. From the crowd an officer emerged and walked onto the stage. "Then why are all these weird creatures popping up all of a sudden? Did you conjure these things with your necromancer powers?"

"Necromancers bring back things from the dead." Antoine said leisurely. "I don't think we found the cure for death yet."

"What my friend here means is that we don't make any creatures," I assured. "They are what we're here to guard you against."

"Well, Mr. SmartyPants, let me show you something," the officer then waved his hand. "Pull down the projector!"

To the left of me descended a white projector screen. It slowly came to a halt about an inch from the ground with a deathly screech. "What is that thing?" the officer asked as a picture of a Calpurtunia appeared on the screen.

Calpurtunia; very dangerous. Known for their long extending claws. They use their barbed tongues to quickly devour plants and small insects. They also use the acid from their tongues to attack enemies when they're provoked. Calpurtunia are mostly bothered by unsuspecting humans in jungles. If exposed to eyes, the acid leaves the prey blind in less than ten seconds.

"Totally harmless," I lied. "Where did you see this creature mister – oh, I didn't really catch your name. Care to tell?"

"I'm Leroy Willis," he stomped his boot. "And it's Officer Willis to you. And we saw this *monster* near The Hideout. Along with this (the screen flicked to a Blat), and this (now to a Rolmermade). I won't ask you again, where did these things come from?"

"They were here the whole time," I started. "We're here to protect them… from you people."

The crowd was now in an uproar. More microphones shoved into our faces. Cameras flashing that blinded our vision. There were too many questions being asked to comprehend. "You *things* are the murderers! All of you!" came a voice. "Witches! Burn the witches!" came another. Police trying to hold down the riot stepped in front of us, holding out their hands. My crew was getting restless and so was I.

"I promise you, we are here to protect!" I stood up. "What is wrong with you people?"

"Don't you think that if we had wanted to hurt you, we would have done so by now?" Jay asked. He and the others were all standing up by now. "Look at us, we're just kids. We want peace!" Then Jay slammed his hand down on the table sending a rush throughout the whole room.

Then, everything froze.

First, every sound was drowned out by the noise the brick wall behind us made when it exploded.

Next, something hard hit my head and back, sending me flying towards the back of the room.

Then, I gathered my senses again and turned my head towards the gaping hole in the wall.

Finally, I heard my old friend, a friend I hadn't heard from in months, Maggie. Her words were simple and full of power, "Oh, but Richard's friend, I don't want peace. I want revenge."

CHAPTER II

Whiplash

Margaret.

Instinctively, I reached for my sword but found out where the cold metal should've lain, there was nothing. "They ambushed us! Open fire!" I heard Officer Willis scream in the midst of the commotion. Great. Quickly standing I checked to make sure everyone was okay. As I passed by Brooke, she grabbed on to my empty hand and I pulled her up.

Brooke's long, brunette hair swished as she rose from the ground. "Thanks," I barely heard her say as I helped her up. At the last second, her hair engulfed my face in a sea of brown beauty. I breathed in as the smell of the ocean filled my nose with familiar memories; Fiona's hair smelt the same way. No surprise though because Brooke and Fiona are water Guardians. I stood still as I fantasized but Brooke's green cat-like eyes snapped everything back into perspective.

Margaret.

"Everyone," I commanded. "Head back to Tensar to fetch your weapons. I have some unfinished business with our party pooper over there. Afterwards, meet me back at the highest building two miles from here."

"Are you crazy?" Jay asked as he got to his feet. "No, I'm coming with you. We're not having another episode, okay?"

"Ooh, and me too," Brooke smiled at me.

"No Brooke," I said calmly. "You stay here and help the rest of them silence all of this commotion. Now everyone know the plan? Good, now head out!"

"But I –" was the last thing I head Brooke say as Jay and I sprinted for Maggie. Margaret must have decided to bring a mini army with her. Her soldiers draped in white robes slithered across the room attacking the humans and my friends. A quick sucker punch to my right sent one of the creeps flying as I kept on running. I glanced to my left and confirmed that Jay was still with me; the target still in sight.

I leaped into the air grabbing for Maggie. A quick flash to her right hit me in the stomach and sent me soaring to the left. Jay quickly followed up with a Fire Frenzy. Maggie, easily dodging the fire, Forced Pushed Jay back into the crowd. From where I laid in the grass, I sensed something was wrong. Maggie never used her Guardian powers; I didn't even know she had Guardian powers. She always used her sword. The last time we met, I had broken it.

11

"Nice of you to join the party," I laughed. "Even though I didn't invite you."

"You on national TV is invitation enough," she glared. "Plus, I think we have some unfinished business to take care of."

"Every party needs a pooper and that's why we invited you," I chanted. Changing my position on the grass, I saw Jay charging for her again. "Party pooper," I laughed as Jay ran into her side, knocking them both to the ground. I took that opportunity to swiftly get to my feet. As the two rolled on the ground, Maggie got the upper hand on Jay and kicked him off with one leg. Jay stumbled and got to his feet just as Maggie got to hers.

"Now this isn't fair," Maggie started.

"That ambush wasn't fair either," Jay grabbed his stomach. "Nor were those kicks, ouch."

"Why are you here Margaret?" I questioned "There's nothing left for you to fight for."

"There is something for me to fight for," she stated. "I want revenge! Tell me where the Crystal is! I know you know where it is. It's just a matter of time before you go get it! Just tell me where it is now and all of this can end!"

"She's crazier than I thought she was," Jay said, flinging his hands in the air. "What are you talking about, lady?"

"You know what I'm talking about, you idiot!" she then turned her head to me. "Why are you hiding it from me, just tell me!"

"Even if I knew where or what this thing is, I wouldn't tell you," I started. "Why would I help you in the first place? Go back to

12

your little hiding place and leave us alone. We don't want any trouble from –"

My rant was stopped because I got the wind knocked out of me. By what, you ask? A figure from the sky, I supposed. All I knew was that it had pinned me down and I was struggling to get out. Then, I looked into the face of the person that had me immobile.

He had tattoos all over his face. His teeth were a sick shade of yellow, close to rotting. His breath was revolting as a dog's. He had a hard face that could make a baby cry by just looking at it. His facial expression, the face of a killer, was in some sort of a frown as if he did not want to be there. I had to find a way out and there was only one way; I spit in his eyes.

Yeah, I know, cheap shot.

As he covered his eyes with his hands, I clapped mines over his ears. Spraying water into his ear canals, the big guy finally fainted while I held his limp head in my hands. Tossing him over to the side, I stood once again facing Maggie and Jay. I looked back down at the huge body and I stepped a few feet over for safety.

"And who is that?" I said pointing to the unconscious body. "Please don't tell me you've been feeding Lunk steroids."

"That's Seth," Maggie started. She then began to sarcastically laugh. "He's been in prison for thirty years doing nothing but lifting weights. Him and Lunk are real good friends, oh yes. It is so sad Lunk couldn't make it to the party, though. He's kinda busy handling some other *dirty* business right now. But enough of this chatter, I believe this fight is fairly matched now if I say so myself."

Side glancing at Jay I gave him a slight twitching signal; Double team attack on primary target. In unison, Jay and I then charged at each other. Quickly cuffing my hands, I spread them out towards Jay's leaping boot. Using almost half of my strength, I accelerated Jay into the clear blue sky. A slight draft passed by my shoulder and I turned in time to block Maggie's attack with a Rock Arm, slightly damaging her forearm.

An underhand jab to my stomach caught me off guard and I flinched. With my free hand, I reached for my utility belt. I felt around for my electrically charged pocketknife and grasped onto the handle. As I thrusted the knife out of my belt, Maggie gave me a head butt. Stumbling backwards, I threw the knife directly at her chest. The knife screamed with electricity as it flew through the air.

As quickly as I had thrown the knife, Maggie rose up her undamaged forearm revealing a bracer. A harmless "ping" echoed throughout the air as the knife tapped the bracer, then fell to the ground with a soft thud.

"I have a lot of tricks up my sleeve as you can see, Richard." Maggie laughed. "We may be peers but you are no match for me. You've gotten lucky these past few encounters. Even without my sword you are no match for me."

"Oh, yeah?" I smiled. "I believe I have a few tricks up my sleeve too." Just as I finished speaking an orange flash appeared in the sky above Margaret. As the flash got bigger and closer, I smiled and said, "Next time, try to get an invitation to the party." Jay, holding onto a fifty meter Fire Hammer ascended upon Maggie. As Maggie looked up her expression changed from happiness to disbelief as Jay's Hammer was inches from her face. Then, my facial expression changed to disbelief. Seth, that giant Lunk clone from earlier, intersected the fire, extinguishing it.

14

Jay and Seth landed next to each other away from Maggie and I. Jumping to my feet, I engaged on Maggie, attacking her with a barrage of Ice Spikes. Gracefully dodging them, Maggie Force Pushed me a few meters away from her as I threw more Ice Spikes. Using some of my stored energy, I teleported behind Maggie and I held onto her neck, giving her little room to breathe.

"Had enough?" I asked.

"Not quite," Maggie said. Then she jabbed me in the stomach. "You idiot." Repeatedly, she continued to thrust her elbow into my stomach, causing me to squeeze harder and harder on her esophagus. Fading in and out of consciousness, I slowly closed my arms around her neck as she continued to bash me with her elbow. Blood rushing to my head, my temple began throbbing. My vision became obscure and I began to fall closer and closer to the ground.

"Rick, can you hear me?" a feminine voice called. "Rick!"

"Who's there?" I said in a daze. "Whadaya want?"

"It's me, Fiona!" the voice said. I wasn't sure if she was real or not but my heart rate increased, I began to sweat, and my head landed hard on the grass. Reality started fading, cutting in and out. Wait, did she say Fiona? Fiona!? My dear, dear Fiona! I thought she was dead. Where is she? With my obscured vision, I looked around. No one but Maggie was in my line of sight.

"Fiona?" I called. "Is that you?"

"I knew you were an idiot," Maggie said as she bent down in front of me. "But not this much of an idiot. She's dead. Dead! And that's what about to be in a minute." Grabbing my shirt, Margaret snatched me off the ground and we met face to face. "Listen, you little runt," she said as I heard something metal slide out

15

of her left arm. "Tell me where the Crystal is and everyone can go home in one piece."

"What Crystal are you talking about?" I struggled to get free.

"The Crystal of Life!" she spit in my face. "I know you know where it is!"

"I have never even heard of that thing!" I yelled. "You're crazy!"

"Fine," Maggie then slid the blade to my neck. "Tell your little girlfriend I said "Hey" for me." Then the cold blade slowly slid across my throat. Little droplets of blood began to form on the edge of the metal. Then, all became still again. All of my sense focused onto my nose. I smelt it, water. Quick, Rick, think fast. Power storage at ten percent.

Got it!

It was risky but I had it.

I narrowed my eyes towards Jay, thought about Jay, then I teleported. Dodging one of Seth's sporadic punches, I looked back towards my enemy. Brooke, carrying onto an eighty meter Water Hammer, slammed the ocean onto an unsuspecting Maggie. Brooke safely landed as the water was sucked into the ground. Maggie's body laid still on the soft grass. Seth, dazzled, ran towards Maggie.

"Let's get out of here!" Brooke said as she landed on the ground. Jay and I exchanged glances at each other and took her advice. Reaching out my arm I Thrust Grabbed Brooke and caught her body in my arms. Fleeing, I looked back and saw Seth hunching over Maggie who seemed unconscious. Not trusting my feet, I doubled forward and sprinted ahead. Glancing up, I saw it, the highest building in my eyesight. I was lucky to make it out of there alive.

"Brooke, I thought I told you to stay with the others," I said as I took another deep breath. We made it to the base of an old office building. Everyone was fine, a few scratches here and there but they all were fine. There was no sign of Seth or Maggie since we high-tailed it out of there. The streets were empty, probably evacuated because of all the commotion down at the conference hall.

"I-I just felt something," Brooke said shyly. "Something terribly wrong. I wanted to see if you were okay, Rick. I didn't know what to think."

"Give her a break," Jay said as he wiped the blood off my neck. "If it wasn't for her you wouldn't have a head, bro. And I wasn't doing so sparkly myself. Seth is a pretty tough opponent, I give him that. Too tough, actually." As Jay finished patching up my neck, I looked towards Brooke. So innocent, but she must have a tough side. Lance must not have even known his own squad very well.

Lance and I have not always been on the friendly side. I could acknowledge that he is the leader of Squad B but when he tries to take over the entire operation, that's not gonna fly. His arrogance for my leadership has kept us both on edge with each other. I'm not ignorant enough to completely ignore him, though. He is a leader and he has those qualities about him but sometimes we don't agree on how things should roll.

"This is exactly what I was talking about, Jay," I started. "Two months of training and we still could have died! We're just kids, it's like we're trying to kill ourselves. We should've just stayed at Bikini Atoll."

17

Yeah, that's right; we stayed at Bikini Atoll for two months. It was perfect; the radiation kept most of the humans away from us. The few humans that were allowed there were to help my friends and I. Tensar put a veil around them to protect them from the radiation. Good thing there was no heat on us so we could have left at anytime we wanted to.

"No," Lance spoke up. "We have to make peace with the humans. They may seem as a little threat to us now but they are capable of harnessing weapons of mass destruction that can even kill Guardians. But, I guess, Maggie has now made it almost impossible to have allies with the humans now. They think Maggie's army is on our side."

"Those *things* were merciless!" Sam insisted. "They were attacking Guardians and the humans, like they had no other will but to kill. They're creepy, just creepy."

"Do you think we'll have to fight them again, Rick?" Brooke asked.

"I don't know," I said to no one in particular. Rolling my neck, I felt the fresh stitches Jay put there. "Hey, Jay, help me up will you?"

Jay, who was standing, reached out his right hand. Grasping it with mine, I felt the symbol on my backhand become hotter. The lighting symbol on my Glove began to glow and so did the fire symbol on his. We both gave each other a quirky smile as I finally stood on my feet. Turning to my friends I said, "I think it's time we leave the Big Apple and go somewhere more tropical." Then I smiled at Brooke. It was time to head back home.

CHAPTER III

Itsy-bitsy, Teeny-weeny, Yellow Polka-dot Bikini Atoll

"I saw what happened on the news," Chris said as Brooke and I stepped onto the dark, sandy beach. "Everywhere you guys go there has to be some trouble, hunh?"

"No, we don't go to trouble," I stated. "Trouble always finds us." Looking down at my bare feet, a crab scuttled over them. I had taken my boots off because it was easier to swim half the Pacific Ocean without them. Brooke and I swam the way but Keith decided he wanted to fly a little bit with Arlene. I don't think Arlene carried him though; maybe he got Dane to give him a piggy back ride.

A lot of things had happed since we moved to Bikini Atoll. For starters, Baton Rouge's School for the Mind, Body and Soul, along with the rest of the Guardian schools, were discovered on Google Maps and had to be relocated to more secure locations. But they really shouldn't be considered schools anymore. The teachers as well as the students are always out on the prowl, wrangling up creatures or ending some disaster or, like in this case, half way across the world in hiding.

When I said *I* was going to find myself, I didn't expect a whole Atoll of people to follow me. But yet, here they are. All of B.R.S.M.B.S is here…yay. Even though there is a multitude of little islands, only five are in use. There is one for each of the four main elements; Fire, Water, Wind and Earth. The fifth island is for my friends and I; Bikini Island. It's a nice little settlement, unexpected, but nice. And don't think that because I said island I meant something huge.

Chris and his girlfriend, Millicent, stayed here too. They were some of the few humans that were allowed here along with my parents. Both Chris's and Millicent's parents died during the Zane Takeover so they had nowhere else to live. Sam and Dane became closer and got together. How cute, hunh? Unexpectedly, though, Keith and Arlene are a couple also. I wasn't sure but I think Antoine and Sabrina have a thing going too. But Jay and I, we were more worried about keeping all of us alive. That's the only thing that really mattered.

Jay and I's relationship had grown since Fiona's death. We had to step up and become the leaders of the group. Intensive study sessions together, dual combat training, and a little more of an understanding of each other, we can communicate almost silently, predicting each other's moves. I'd say we were the ones that had to do the most growing up. But I had a little more of an extra burden than he did.

"We should wait for the others," Brooke suggested. "Then we should head to Master for a debriefing."

"Yeah," I confirmed. "I have a whole lot to tell him. Hey, Chris, when is that super secret project of yours gonna be finished?" Chris was a engineer, a good one at that. That's the primary reason I wanted him to come there. Ever since we arrived he promised to make my friends and I something special. Who knows what his strange mind could come up with.

"Almost," Chris said. "Working out the kinks." In the distance, tiny specks began to come into eyesight. As the orange sunset reflected over the water, the three of us sat in the sand as our friends flew closer to us. Brooke, with her hand over mine, was completely mesmerized by the beautiful sight. The sea, the water, Brooke; they all reminded me of Fiona.

"Rough winds, Rick." Antoine stated as he touch downed on the beach. "We better head inside." Being an Elemental Guardian, possessing all of the elements, I overlook a lot of things single and dual Guardians can sense in a heartbeat. I can single out an element at will but I wouldn't know which one I would need so I just try to balance all of them. But controlling all of the elements does have its advantages.

"Right," I said. "As soon as everyone arrives we head to Master to see what else we need to do." Fiddling with my right side, I twiddled with my sword. My sword! If I would have had my sword I could have easily defeated Maggie. Now I had something she didn't. I kept a mental note to always keep my toys to myself; they might save my life one day.

Everyone arrived a little bit before the wind and rain started getting too bad. The beach, already empty when we arrived, was on the other side of the island from Master's dwelling. We found Master while traveling the world searching for somewhere to live in peace. Him and his wife were artifact collectors in Egypt but he

21

refused to leave us behind once we found him. His wife stayed behind but Master traveled with us to here, despite his old age.

When I opened the door to Master's home, I spotted Headmaster Ravenhawl and him discussing something in the living room. They both smiled as my whole posse entered and Headmaster Ravenhawl greeted us with a warm, "Ah, welcome home, brave warriors! Take a seat anywhere you like, you deserve it." Me, not wanting to speak, I waited for the rest of them to sit down and crowd the living room, forcing me to sit on the wooden floor Indian style.

"You all returned safely as I expected," Master started. "But, as always, there were a few complications at the conference."

"Yeah, a whole army at that." Lance said stiffly. "They weren't lackeys either. Those things were Guardians or had Guardian powers."

"If they had Guardian powers then they had to be Guardians, right?" Sam asked.

"No, those things weren't even human," Lance corrected. "I could tell by the way they fought."

"There are many things that can harness the power of Guardians," Master started. "They could have been Goblins, clay or stone soldiers or maybe even doppelgangers. This world is full of creatures that we Guardians have yet to understand. That's the challenge, protecting something that we have no idea what we're protecting."

"Just be careful everywhere you go," Ravenhawl warned. "A lot of people, and things, want us dead. Keep your heads up and report back tomorrow evening for your training." With that, we all rose in unison. Ravenhawl stayed with Master in his house as I closed the door behind me.

I walked down the road towards Jay and Brooke who waited on me. Jay said a joke and Brooke burst out laughing before I arrived. That Jay, international funny man.

"Goodnight," Brooke waved as she headed towards her cabin with Sabrina. I waved to her goodnight then Jay and I headed towards our cabin. Why Jay? Because he doesn't care who he bunks with and by the rules everyone must be in fifty feet of another person at all times. So who better to bunk with than my vice president?

"That girl, Brooke, you like her don't you?" Jay questioned as he captured another one of my pawns. Chess was my favorite pastime (that and eating). It kept my mind sharp and helped with battle strategies. Millicent gave it to me because she thought I needed something to do in my free time. Well, you can't really play chess by yourself now, can you? But as it turns out, Jay likes it too so we play it when we're bored.

"Nah," I said as I protected my queen. "I don't have time for all of that when I'm worried about if she's gonna survive or not."

"Well, she talks to you a lot," Another one of my pawns gone.

"Maybe she's being nice," Forced to move my queen.

"They're all nice, aren't they?" Jay said as he captured my queen. "Checkmate."

"Lucky," I said as I stood from the table. Raiding the kitchen, I grabbed two slices of meat lovers' pizza, an orange drink, and sat down in front of the TV. After cleaning off the chess table, Jay took a seat in the recliner. Throwing him the pizza I said, "Make yourself useful and warm this up for me."

"Why can't you do it?" Jay asked as he warmed my pizza with his hands.

"I'm feeling a bit watery today," I laughed as I drank some orange drink. Turning on the TV, I searched through the channels. We had all of the channels in the world, thanks to the wind Guardians. Every TV is connected by wind to the wind Guardians' island and then they send a signal to the space satellites to beam down onto all of Bikini Atolls' "Boob Tubes".

"Here's your stupid pizza," Jay said as he handed me my plate. I laughed and offered him a slice. Grabbing one, he repeatedly set it on fire, a habit he had gotten into lately. Ever since we could use our powers freely, all of our daily lives have been easier. If I could control the lighting element at will then the whole island would have unlimited electricity too. But to get power we have to wait until a storm comes through and harness the electricity or get wind and water Guardians to make some.

Once the channel turned to NBC, take a guess at what I saw. They must have those news helicopters under some cloaking devices now because I never spot them. Footage of whole event showed with the caption "THEY'RE HERE TO TAKE OVER!!" written under it. Great, there goes our chance with being allies with the humans. The commentator even made it look like my entire crew was the bad people too even though I didn't see any of them attack a human.

"I'm going to bed," I told Jay after I had enough.

"Same," Jay said as he stood. "We got some learnin' to do in the morn', Rick. Best we do head onto bed." He didn't have to tell me twice.

My room was the place where I could collect my thoughts and relax. Lying on my bed, I recalled that days' events. The conference, Maggie, the strange soldiers, Seth...

Fiona.

Was that really her that spoke to me? It sounded like her but I wasn't really sure. That brought me back to the time when I was Zane's prisoner and she spoke to me through that puddle. I never even got the chance to ask her how she did that. But if that was really her that spoke to me, I would like to know how. How was the question that I wanted answered. Well, I wanted to know how a lot of things were but they were too complicated for me to understand. Maybe that was one of those things. I just wished that she would talk to me again.

And Brooke.

Jay had a point when he said that we talked a lot. Yeah, we do talk a lot. But something was in the back of my head driving me forward to talk to her. Was it her hair that smelled like the ocean? Or was it her eyes that reminded me of Fiona's? Her accent...I love accents. The way she dresses, her style, her physique, her everything. Was Brooke a sign that it was time for me to move on? Maybe so, but I wasn't the one to give in so easily. But Brooke was...perfect. She was equally matched with Fiona. But Fiona was dead. Did that mean that I loved Brooke by default?

It must. It had to. I worry a lot as you can see. I'm probably gonna have stress marks when I'm older. Probably not even that long. I needed sleep though. Even heroes need rest.

Snuggling into my bed, I soared into the darkness that I liked to call sleep...

CHAPTER IV

Respect Your Elders

"Rise and shine, princess," Jay yelled as he knocked on my door.

"Stop that," I insisted.

Sunday, July 29th, 2068. Bikini Island, Bikini Atoll. The roof of my mouth was hurting for some reason. Straggling out of bed, I headed towards my clothes. Licking the roof of my mouth repeatedly, I realized that I was bleeding. Ignoring that, I threw on my clothes, grabbed my sword and headed out the door.

"You know," Jay started. "For being the quote, unquote 'leader' of this group, you get up pretty late."

"I have more on my mind than you do," was my simple answer. "Plus, I was always a late sleeper, remember?"

"Oh, I remember," said Jay as we transitioned outside. "You being late for breakfast sometimes and starving in class. Funny."

"Well at least I can go six days without eating anything," I bragged as I swallowed some blood.

"You call *that* an achievement?" Jay started. "More like an achievement you'd get on one of those primitive Xbox's my grandfather used to play. Again, I laugh. Hah."

"You always have to one up me, do you?" I questioned.

"Of course," he said with pride. "Who else would dare to challenge the Great Elemental Guardian?"

"A lot of people," I thought. We walked the rest of the way to the fighting grounds in silence. I admired the beautiful trees and the forever-omniscient sun on the horizon. Since the day we arrived at that place I wondered how something so magnificent could have been used for such dangerous things. But then again, magic is the most powerful thing in the universe.

Master, Ravenhawl, and the rest of the gang were waiting on Jay and I when we arrived. No, we weren't late, we were quite early, actually. The silent piece of code that we Guardians lived by was promptness. If someone said six A.M then we would be there at five. With us, there is no arriving late because that could mean the difference between life and death.

"Okay everyone," Ravenhawl started. "Up until now I have been at every training session with you all. That is because your group of Guardians are the ones that Richard trusts the most and therefore you are the ones appointed to protect him. With that being said, I have taken it that you all would get special training. Well, now the time has come for me to attend to the rest of the island because I am still the Headmaster and I have an obligation to fulfill as such. However, someone more suited of teaching you all has seen you progress and will gladly continue teaching you all. Master, will you please?"

"Yes, very well," Master said as he grabbed our attention. "As you all know, my name is Master."

"I have a question," Sam said. "I know you are very skilled and everything, but why are you called Master?"

"Hm, are you maybe the Master that we have heard about?" Lance pondered.

What Lance was talking about was an entry in our history textbook. If you ask me, I think some of that stuff in there isn't the full truth. I try to make my own assumptions about the Guardian world. They don't even have anything about maintaining the lightning element. But if you were wondering what Master Lance was talking about, here's the entry:

"Before the 2000's, there was born a very young man whose name history does not recall. This young individual was a castaway, orphaned at such an early age that he has no recollection of his parents or his heritage. In the year of 2010, this young warrior's gift was unrevealed, becoming the only living Elemental Guardian, with Diminicus the First dying in 1997. Knowing this, the young warrior went into hiding. Only communicating with the creatures, the young warrior learned the ways of a Guardian, not revealing himself to the world.

"In the year 2020, The Elemental War began. The Elemental War was a war fueled by hatred. Up to the events that lead to the war, fire Guardians and wind Guardians favored each other and

29

water Guardians and earth Guardians favored each other. The tense games that the sides played went out of hand, thus starting the war.

"For five long years, terror filled the world as the Guardians battled with each other showing no mercy. Thousands upon thousands of Guardians died for their element making the population of the Guardians dwindle. There would have been no end until one side extinguished the other. Then, in the winter of 2025, the young warrior revealed himself to the world.

"Controlling all of the elements and the lightning element, he stopped the war. Without killing a single person, the warrior negated all attacks and defeated every warrior. To this day, no one but he himself knows how he did it. Once all the fighting ceased, the Guardians realized their terrible ways. The warrior was praised and was given the title Master for he would not speak his name.

"Eventually, Master found a young maiden whom he wished to marry. The young maiden and Master set off once again from the rest of the world in 2027, never to be seen again."

Of course our Master wasn't the textbook Master. I think I would've been able to distinguish another Elemental Guardian. I sensed him in Egypt. He's so old that he forgot to hide his signal and I picked up on it. That clever devil was in disguise for some reason. I never cared to ask and it wasn't any of my business. But he knew who I was and wanted to enhance my powers. And now, there we were.

"You can call me whatever you want," Master stated. "But, you must listen to everything I say."

"Yes, Master," we all said in unison.

"Very well," Ravenhawl said. "I must be off now. Have fun and please learn something!" Then he teleported to wherever he was headed.

"Line up facing me," Master commanded. "I want fire Guardians first, then earth, wind, water and finally Richard." Following his orders, I took my place at the back of the line next to Brooke. Guardian by Guardian, Master analyzed them with his all-knowing eyes and his experienced vibe.

Finally getting to me, Master analyzed me from head to toe. Being this close I felt the power he possessed, far greater than my own. It seemed even a couple of times I felt one of my elements become stronger then back to normal at rapid paces. Finally, after what felt like hours, Master pulled back and faced us.

"It seems I have a fine group of protégé's in front of me," Master commented. "Since we're not in a rush, what is the first thing that you wish to learn?"

"Fighting, sir," Lance spoke up.

"Hm, why so?" Master questioned.

"Because," Lance smiled. "I love playing with fire."

"Well, does everyone agree?" Master asked.

We all nodded in approval.

"Wonderful," Master said with a hint of laughter, "I love playing with fire too."

CHAPTER V

Playing With Fire

"Alright," Master started. "All fire Guardians, including Richard, step up towards me." Reluctant, my companions and I stepped forward. Remembering all of Mr. Frey's lessons, I calmed myself. The fire element never came naturally to me so I only used it when it was really necessary. Being the hardest one for me to control, I didn't feel comfortable starting off the day with fire. I don't even like matches.

"Now, the ones who cannot use the fire element will be defending in this exercise while the ones who can will try to lightly burn you on a non vital area by simply tapping you." Master explained. Then, the old man split into two. It's a type of mirage advanced wind Guardians can use. I can't do it because it requires a whole reserve of strength.

"I will be teaching the defenders," said one of the Masters.

"And I will teach the attackers," said the other.

Splitting us halfway across the beach, I followed my group with our Master. I realized that I didn't really fight alongside Lance that much as well as Arlene. I remember Arlene as the first fire Guardian I encountered using a fire move up close. That reminded me; I needed to go somewhere after this was over.

Lance, well I didn't really know Lance all that well. It seemed even without us speaking directly that much we had grown a silent relationship. His short, stocky figure didn't match his status as Squad B's leader. His magical whip was a mystery to me, and so were many Guardian weapons. Even my sword I did not know a whole lot about.

"Lance," I said gazing at him. "Where did you get that whip?"

"It was a gift," he said. "From my dad. It was his when he was a Guardian. Said he found it in a cave."

"Oh," I said almost silently. "How does it work? You know, just in case I need to know; emergency or something."

"I don't really know," he said looking down at it. "I just surge my magic in it and it just catches on fire. Never really cared how it worked. As long as it burns, I'm good."

We made it to our destination, far away from the others. As instructed, we placed our utility belts and weapons in the sand in front of us. We were using bare hand attacks.

"Rick, give me your hand," Master commanded. Gazing down, Master stared at my Power Glove with his hard, all-knowing eyes. "I see my Power Gloves have been of good use to you. I'm going to ask you all to remove them."

Taking off both of my gloves, I suddenly felt weaker. Two months of training and I felt little change in my power supply. With the Gloves, I was barely a match for Maggie; how would it have gone if I didn't have the Gloves? Looking at my bare, brown backhands, my piece of the symbol stood out and so did Jay's.

"Permanent as I said before," Master said referring to Jay and I's symbols. "That's a very powerful spell you two have."

"It's an honor to have it," Jay said smartly.

"As you must honor the dead, young Guardian," Master stated. "Today, I shall teach you all the Sacred Fire Fairy Technique. Not commonly taught at this level but I am pretty sure you all can handle it. Other than today, I do not want you to try to attempt this Technique unless it is highly necessary. Not only could you danger yourself, you could also damage the environment. Also, there is a slight chance you might not leave out of the transformation."

"Transformation?" I asked.

"Yes, you will all turn into Fairies, Fire Fairies to be exact." Master said.

Fairies are weird things. Some are calm and others are bent on destruction. We were taught how to spot and avoid any kind of Fairy. They were sent to Earth by an unknown force to harness the elements. The thought of even turning into one made me shudder with fear. But I was curious on how I could turn into a fairy…

"Sounds fun," Arlene said sarcastically.

"There are only two things I must teach you before you try to transform into a Fire Fairy: How to find your Fire Fairy and how to control it. They are both very simple tasks but the latter is the most crucial."

"Why is that, Master?" I asked.

"Because Fire Fairies are cruel and heartless and will try to overtake your soul if you're not strong enough."

"…creepy," Lance said.

"Very," Master agreed. "But no worries, I will monitor you the whole time so it shall not happen even if you make a mistake. Now, to find the Fairy, you must close your eyes and search inside yourself. Once you're there I will know and continue teaching individually."

I was pretty sure I had searched inside of myself plenty of times before. Closing my eyes, I stared into the cold darkness of my inner eyelids. Nothing. Come on, concentrate, Rick. Rick. Richard Raines. Fire. Think. Then without warning, my ears shut down. Next, the sand under my feet was gone and I was completely alone.

I opened my eyes and saw nothing but darkness. Turning my head, I realized everything was exactly the same, darkness. I reached out my hands to feel for something, anything, and I found nothing. It seemed like it would be like that for the rest of eternity… and I was scared.

I stayed scared; I didn't know what I had to do. I must move, I thought. So I began to kick my feet, swimming actually. I will admit, it was kinda fun. I try to make the best out of everything so I stayed calm. By calm I meant almost freaking out but I was good. I was good.

After what seemed like a millennium, four very small dots of color appeared out of the darkness. Acknowledging this achievement, I swam faster, every second the dots becoming larger. Soon, I could recognize that each dot was a different color: red, blue, brown and white. The white stood prominently out in the darkness.

Excited, I swam more rapidly. Approaching the four dots, I realized that they were massive spheres. As I floated closer and closer, I realized something. I could feel them. They were alive. But they were omniscient, not moving since I arrived. But strangely they were calling me, all four of them. The sounds, the invisible gestures made me linger closer. I was so close to the blue one, about to touch it.

"Don't," Master's voice boomed.

"Master?" I questioned. "Where are you?"

"I'm still on the beach. I stayed in contact with your mind. Don't touch the blue one." he commanded.

"Why?" I asked. "I feel like I have to, I want to."

"Exactly," he started. "That is why you must not touch it. You are a special case because you have all of the elements. Each sphere represents an element. There is a twist to all of them. The water sphere lured you with lust, which is its power. That is for another day. You may not fool with it today. But you may touch the red one. Go ahead, I'm here."

Drifting away from the voice of the blue orb, I headed towards the red one. The red one's energy felt more fierce and unfamiliar than the blue. The red one actually made me scared. I wanted to touch the blue one but not this one. But red must have stood for fire. Of course, it all made sense. What else would it stand for? Slowly and cautiously, I reached my hand out. Then I touched it.

I jerked my hand back because suddenly the orb burst into flames. Slowly, the orb became smaller; a figure was starting to become defined. First, the head came into play, small and twitching. Next came the body, muscular and slim. Still on fire, the figure opened its red piercing eyes. I had seen an Earth Fairy in textbooks because they were the less creepy of the species. But the Fire Fairy was something out of a nightmare.

"So…you came," the Fairy said with an evil voice.

"…," I swallowed my bloody spit.

"Don't be afraid, Richard," Master warned. "Intimidation is his trick. Tell him you want to use him as a shield, nothing else."

"What, are you scared?" The Fairy asked. "Scaredy cats are such pushovers."

"I'm not scared," I lied. "I want you to be my shield."

"Be your shield?" the Fairy started floating towards me. "But Richard, we hardly know each other." He cackled. "Of course, I know you. But do you even know my name?"

"Fairies have names?" I asked.

"Do the disgusting little creatures we call humans have names?" the Fairy asked as it placed its hand on my shoulder. Then it laughed a menacing laugh, spreading its fiery mouth. "In the human tongue I am known as Thero. But you can call me Mr. T. Ha!"

"Great," I said. "Thero, I need you to do me a favor."

"Yeees?" Thero asked.

"Can you be my shield?" I asked. "Only my shield until I say otherwise."

"Hmm," Thero said as he floated around me. "I don't know if I can do that."

"Be more aggressive," Master suggested.

"Thero," I started. Facing my fears, I faced fear in the face. "You are inside of me. I control you. There is no way you will win this argument. I don't even know you, you don't have to be so stingy."

"You are greatly mistaken, dear Richard," Thero sizzled. "Who do you think you are?"

"I am," I gained some more confidence. "I am Rick Raines. Thero, I'm not gonna ask you again. Be my shield; NOW!" I don't know where I got all of those guts from.

I heard sort of a sigh from Thero. "If you insist," Thero said cocking his head to the side. Moving his head back and opening his mouth, Thero began to stand still. As I stared into the empty darkness of his mouth, I became scared again. He was just standing there and Master wasn't saying anything. Then, in a slow movement, Thero fixed his head and stared at me with his mouth still gaping open. Finally, Thero lurched forward and I entered the darkness of his mouth.

I began to scream my lungs out. I was burning, BURNING! Nevertheless, as I burned I noticed something. I could feel my knees in the sand. The sand! Quickly opening my eyes, I realized that I was burning from the inside out. My skin turning to a crisp as the skin

38

cells were being replaced by fire. Screaming in pain, I turned to my side and saw the same process happening to the other fire Guardians. The pressure in my head began to rise and I felt nothing. No burning anymore. I checked my skin; I was still on fire.

"It feels good, doesn't it?" Thero asked from inside my head.

"What is this?" was my response.

"It's what you asked for," Thero laughed. "You're wearing me."

Standing up I realized that I had became shorter, lighter. I felt Master's presence monitoring me from inside my head. It seemed as if Thero knew he was there but did not want to engage with the Guardian. Standing on my toes, I began to float in the air and I began to feel free. As the other three Fairies floated near me, I could not tell who was who.

"Which one of you is which?" I asked unexpectedly in Thero's voice.

"Jay Alonso reporting for duty," the one in the middle said.

"I don't know who or what I am now but I was once called Lance," said the other one on the right.

"And I'm Arlene obviously," came a voice from the left.

"Right, now Master, what are we suppose to do?" I asked.

"Lightly tap all of the other Guardians!" Master yelled from the ground.

Without further conversation, we headed out. Flying as a Fire Fairy was weird. Thero's sporadic movements did not go well under

39

my control. Twisting and turning, we swiftly approached the rest of the Guardians. I could sense their battle strategy as I flew closer. The water Guardians were evenly spread out throughout the group to quickly power us down.

"Aim as closely as you can to one of the water Guardians but land in the sand!" I yelled to the others. We watched in wonder as the other Guardians spotted us. Fear on their faces, they readied their selves for our fast approach. Only two water Guardians and four Fire Fairies . That was going to go badly for them.

Jay and Thero, following my commands, headed straight for Brooke. Arlene and Lance headed for Keith who face was in fear. Brooke, thinking she dodged us, quickly moved to the side and my hot flesh hit the sand. Falling into a barrel roll I quickly floated again while Jay flew on the other side of Brooke. Then, as Brooke twirled to face me, she smiled.

Suddenly, my body jerked back as Thero saved me from an earth hammer. Aiming upwards, I flew towards Sabrina's hovering body. Kicking me in the face with her earth shoes, Sabrina was flown off by Sam who was holding her the whole time. Retaliating, I hurtled towards Sabrina's chest. Lightly tapping Sabrina with the pointer finger of my left hand then reaching for Sam with the other, I quickly flew above them.

"Out!" I said in Thero's cruel voice.

With only Brooke, Dane, Keith and Antoine left I felt confident since it was fairly matched. Scanning the area, I spotted Lance and Dane going at it, Dane blocking all of Lance's attacks. Thero did not give me any more time to look and headed straight for Dane for a sneak attack. Then I noticed that Thero was aiming to knock the wind out of Dane.

Taking control of my own body, I swerved out of the way just in time to barely miss Dane's back. Instead of hitting Dane, I hit Lance. Spinning towards the sand, Dane took that chance to trap us in an earth dome. The flames from the Fairies gave us light in the dome but otherwise it was darkness. Getting up off the sandy ground, I looked at Lance.

"You're an idiot, Rick," Thero said aloud.

"You were going to hurt him!" I yelled. "What is wrong with you?"

"I was being your shield, remember?" Thero said matter-of-factly.

"Hey!" yelled Lance or Lance's Fairy. "We should be thinking of a way to get out of here, not arguing."

"Simple," Thero said. Reaching my arms out, I stuck them in the sand, burning it. "We can just burn our way through."

"Do you wanna go first, Thero?" Lance's Fairy obviously said. "Because I remember the last time I trusted you, I almost died."

"That was a mistake and you know that," Thero said. "And yeah, I'll go first." Not expecting to move so fast, I was surprised to feel my head go into the sand, setting it on fire. Next, I placed my hands next to me accelerating the process of burning the sand. Eventually, Lance joined in and we started to burn a hole.

Being completely covered in sand with no oxygen, I was forced to hold my breath and let Thero take control of the operation. I had been practicing holding my breath before to swim longer so it wasn't that big of a challenge. Soon enough, Thero came bursting out on the other side of the dome, filling oxygen back into my lungs.

41

A little while afterwards, Lance came bursting out of the sand on my side.

Turning towards Master, I saw that Keith and Antoine were eliminated while we were incarcerated. Over to the side it was Jay and Arlene against Dane and Brooke. Knowing it would be an easy win, Lance and I headed towards the fight, eager to get it over with. We didn't have to sneak up on them because they were outmatched anyhow and their loss was in the foreseeable future. Colliding head to head with Dane, I was thrusted back by his powerful earth arm. Back and forth, Dane and I traded powerful blows that did nothing but weaken us both.

"It seems we are at a standstill, earth Guardian," Thero said as Dane and I collided again. "You are lucky I am not at my full power, otherwise this would have been child's play."

"I'm stronger than I look," Dane said. "And I think I'm pretty strong." Then Dane stomped his foot on the sand. A low rumble erupted from the Earth below my feet, then, as quick as lightning; I was shot into the air by the sand that ruptured under me. Stabling myself, I quickly searched the clear blue sky. Then it almost hit me.

"Watch it!" Thero said as he flew my body backwards, dodging Dane's Earth Hammer. "I'm so tired of this!" Suddenly, Thero rocketed towards Dane. The scene below was chaotic. Jay was trying to get an advantage on Brooke while Dane was aiming to fight the other two Fairies. The hatred in Thero's being was so strong that it was slowly seeped into mine. Thero was trying to completely take control over my body so I fought back. Mentally attacking each other, my body was at a standstill. Then for a split second, I got the upper hand.

Landing inches from Dane, I stretched my foot out to stop advancing towards him. Feeling my feet meet the back of Dane's feet, I pushed my legs forward and tripped him. Thero then took the upper hand and returned to control my body. Since I was already in the sand, he pounced for Brooke's stomach. With my arms aimed at her stomach, it was going to be a fatal blow. Straining my mind, I fought Thero again. Knowing I could not easily best him that time, I tricked him.

For a split second, I acted as if I had the same intentions as Thero did. Together we aimed for Brooke's stomach with equal control. Then I pounced on Thero's consciousness, gaining me access to my body. Retracting my arms, I flew to the right. Then as I swerved around, I saw Brooke make her escape. Keeping control of my own body, I flew towards the other Fairies .

"You fool!" Jay's Fairy yelled. "You were right there at the kill! How could you let a *human* change your course."

"He likes to play mind games," Thero started. "I see your human has you under control as well so you have no room to talk."

"I have plenty, Thero!" Jay's Fairy said. "You bring disgrace to our race. You're quite shameful, actually."

"Shameful?!" Thero questioned. "What I do and what I have done in the past was for the greater good of this race. And what do I get? I get to be trapped in a disgusting little human! You should be shamed!" Then without realizing it, Thero spat my mouth full of blood onto the chest of Jay. Then, a dreadful silence fell over all of the Fairies. My blood then began to slowly crawl around Jay's body, creating a spider web of blood across his body.

"Oops," Thero apologized. "My bad."

"Everyone back away!" Master said as Jay let out a yell to the heavens. "Now!"

Hearing Master's command, I realized that I was immobile. Brooke and the rest headed back to Master leaving me alone with Jay. The blood had fused with the fire, causing Jay's skin to look more menacing than before. Moving away from the blood, I stared into Jay's eyes. Even though they were red before, they now had no soul behind them. I didn't see my best friend behind those eyes.

"Jay?" I said as I flew a little closer. In the back of my head, Thero told me to not approach him. Not listening, I reached out my arm. A powerful blow landed in the middle of my chest, sending me back a few hundred feet. I was Force Grabbed by someone in mid air and I was slowly brought to the rest of the group. Thero's skin protected me, for I could feel that it was somehow damaged.

"Master, what's going on?" Arlene asked in her normal voice.

"Something very, very terrible." Thero answered. "Something that only happens when I screw up."

"What do you mean, Fairy?" Antoine questioned.

"He means," Master started. "Jay has become a Fire Blood Fairy."

CHAPTER VI

True Friends

"Can someone please explain what *that thing* is?" Dane ordered. "It's just floating there looking all creepy."

"It's finishing the ritual," Thero said. "Not much longer now."

"A ritual for what exactly?" Lance asked.

"To complete the transformation," Master said. "We must stop it before it begins. Thero, you may be knowledgeable on the subject but you will be no help in defeating it. I'm afraid I am going to have to put you back inside Richard."

"Fine," Thero said after a second. "Farewell, puny humans. Best of luck to you all. You're gonna need it." As Thero laughed, Master slowly receded Thero back into my body, transforming me to normal. Or as normal as I was going to get. Looking down at my brown skin and feeling full control over my body again, I stood next to Master and Brooke. Then I looked back at Jay... that wasn't Jay.

"Richard, come with me," Master commanded. "The rest of you stay back. The things that are needed to be done can only be done by an Elemental Guardian."

I sprinted behind Master to follow his lead. For an old man he ran pretty fast. Then again, Guardians life spans are longer. Our skin advances at the same pace as humans but the inside prolongs itself. But knowing myself, I'm probably going to die young from all the Meat Lover's Pizza I eat.

"I'm right behind you, Master," I said as we sprinted even closer to the Fire Blood Fairy. Master pointed me to spilt and go on the right side on the Fairy as he went to the left. One hundred meters apart from the Fairy, we stopped and looked at each other. Not knowing what to do, I waited for Master's command. The omniscient Fairy stood just there, ignoring us as if we weren't even there.

"Richard," Master spoke to me in my mind. "I'm going to teach you something through telepathy, for if the Fairy knew of our plans it would try to stop them."

"Gotcha," I replied in my head. Telepathy was a wind Guardian power that I had not yet learned. But I did know that if a wind Guardian was talking to you through telepathy they could hear your speech thoughts.

"So what we are going to do is make seals," Master said.

"Seals?" I asked. "Are we going to try to trap it?"

"Exactly. We're each going to make a seal for each element including lighting," Master explained. "Do you know how to make a seal?"

"No," I answered. Creating seals is an ancient technique. They were a Guardian's magical presence left on a physical object to protect or restrain something. They sap your energy every time they are used so Guardians who have placed seals that are long forgotten or cannot be destroyed have to carry the burden of not knowing when the seal would be needed. "I never had the need to make one."

"This is going to be tricky then," Master said. "Have you expelled pure magic from your hands before?"

"Not that I recall," I said. "It's such a tricky thing so I never learned it."

"I figured," Master said with a groan. "It's like flamethrowers from your hand. But instead of harnessing your fire magic, you don't add anything to it. Make it bland."

"Okay," I answered. "Then what?"

"Then concentrate it on the sand in a circle," he explained. "Then switch to the fire element and follow me from there."

It was hard to think about no elements but still generate magic. Everything I had learned up to that point involved one of the five elements. I was pretty sure that seals were the only thing that didn't require any of them. So that should have made it easy, right? No, once you learned a certain way to do something then that's the easiest way for you. But doing something new and hard stimulates your brain and makes you a smarter person.

I was feeling really dumb right then. Aiming my hands towards the sand, I sent a surge of fire to my hands. Make the magic bland, I thought. Like crawfish without seasoning. So what could negate the fire? Water. I just had to extinguish the fire and all I would have left is pure magic. Bravo, Richard, I thanked myself. Then I happily added water to the equation.

Letting the pure energy escape my hands, I created a circle around me. Beaming pure white, I felt my magic connected to the empty seal.

"Great," Master commended. "Now make four more." On and on I continued to make the seals. The process became easier but I felt my energy deplete from using fire and water so much. The Fairy continued to make its presence unknown by staying in its trance. Once all of the seals were in place, Master and I stood in the seals closest to the Fairy.

"Come, all of you," Master called out with his mind. "But speak only with your minds."

"Yes, Master," I heard Sam and Antoine say.

"Just as Richard and I are facing each other," Master started. "I want the elements facing each other. No less than one to a circle. Quickly, before the Fairy finishes its ritual. Water Guardians first, then wind, then earth, then fire." Gathering in the circles, Brooke stood in the closest to me. Suddenly, I felt the lightning element surge through me. Then I remembered I had left my Power Gloves meters away.

"I unlocked the lightning, Richard," Master spoke to me. "You're going to need it."

"How did you do that?" I asked. The lightning element felt good.

"You will find out your own way to use it at your own will," Master said. "If I told you, you wouldn't appreciate it as much. Right, now everyone, elemental blast the empty seals you're standing in."

Lightning now engulfing me, I focused it into the palm of my hands. Without looking down, I surged the lighting in the seal. As I did so, I felt the others do the same, connecting me to the Guardians who were using my seals. All of their energy and magic were at my disposal. A white line of pure magic then connected all of my seals to form a chain.

"Now, Richard," Master started. "Connect you lightning with my magic through the Fairy. Remember: Fire for friendly, Water for pain, Earth for control and Wind for force. Ready? Everyone brace yourselves! Go!"

Using my whole body as a producer, I attacked the Fairy. Suddenly, the Fairy became conscious. My first thought was to begin slamming it with water. When I connected with Master, I felt that Jay was still in there. Then the thought of killing him crossed my mind and I switched to fire.

The Fairy began attacking us. Mentally, it had the strength of a thousand Guardians. Physically, I didn't want to think of what it could do physically. We just had to hold him until all of its energy depleted. The attacks seemed endless as if it was never going to stop. Rushing wind into my magic, it slowed a little bit but then became stronger.

"This isn't working!" I said. "It's stronger than all of us combined."

"Keep going!" Master yelled.

Suddenly, the Fire Blood Fairy pierced our ears with its screech. Not knowing what to do, I broke the connection with Master. Everyone flew back as the terrible creature yelled in horror. Suddenly being brave, I ran towards the creature, aiming to attack it. Electrically charging my hands, I pinned electricity through the Fairy's chest.

The Fairy was unaffected and easily knocked me off its chest. Staggering back to my feet, I quickly rushed behind it. I wasted no time uprooting the earth beneath the Fairy's feet, causing it to hover a few feet in the air. Then, with its soulless eyes, it turned to face me. In shock, I staggered a back a few steps. Aware of my mistake, the Fairy closed in on me.

"Foolish mortal," it said in a horrendous voice. "Now you shall be the first to perish in my rein." Dumbfounded, I stood there like an idiot. With a defining roar, the Fairy plunged after me with its fiery hand extended. As I tried to cover my face up, I thought I was going to see Fiona…

But I didn't die. How would I be saying this if I did? Peeking through my arm, the Fairy was knocked to my right by two blurs. The Fairy and the two blurs landed on the sand a few meters away. Brooke and Dane continued to attack the creature. Snapping back into reality, I rushed into the fight. The Fairy grabbed Dane and Brooke by their shirts as I approached them. Not being able to do anything, the Fairy head butted them together and they fell to the ground.

I grabbed onto the Fairy's neck as I rushed into him. Twisting around, I planted my feet into its back. Jerking back, we landed on the ground becoming a flaming cartwheel. Trying to land punches while you were spinning was a challenge. As the Fairy burned my skin for the fiftieth time, I threw it off of me. I landed quietly in the sand right next to my Power Gloves.

I quickly assembled the special leather onto my hands. I felt my power enhance and the lightning flew to the Gloves. Sprinting once again with new energy, I collided with the creature again. Using the same tactic as before, I swung my hands around its neck. Grabbing onto its torso with my legs, I let go of its neck.

Generating more electricity, I created Lightning Bolts in my hand. With no remorse, I jabbed them into the back of the Fairy. As the Fairy screamed in pain, I shoved them in further.

"Jay," I started. "I know you're in there. Come on, man!"

"HE'S NOT HERE!" the Fairy yelled. "YOU CANNOT DEFEAT ME!"

"SHUTUP, YOU DON'T KNOW HIM, FAIRY!" I began sending more lightning into its back. "JAY, COME OUT!"

"NEVAH! – I'm here, Rick! – NO YOU'RE NOT!" The Fairy and Jay screamed.

"I'M COMING, JAY!" I pushed the bolts further into its back.

Then the lightning bolts gave in. I jumped off the back of the Fairy and watched in fascination. The Fairy yelled a blood-curdling scream that was so horrible that I had to cover my ears. Slowly, the fire and molten skin on Jay transformed back into his white skin.

Then, the white of his eyes could be seen along with his pupils. I watched as if a DVD was being fast-forwarded as hair grew back on Jay's now normal head.

Jay was on his knees as the transformation completed. I was the first one to reach him and I knelt beside him. Patting him on his back, he coughed up some blood. He then looked at me with an expression of sadness on his face. I nodded for I could only imagine what he had been through in those minutes. The others arrived by then and I shooed them away to give Jay some space.

"You okay, buddy?" I asked, patting him on the back again.

"I don't know," he said. "I can't feel anything and I'm half blind."

"Only a few side effects," Master said. "We should get you somewhere to rest." Gathering up some of my strength, I lifted Jay off the ground. The sea of Guardians parted as I carried my best friend off the beach. Like little kids following the line leader, Master and the Guardians stayed close behind.

Dane slowly opened the door to my hut to let me in. I carefully laid Jay down in his bed and let Sam tuck him in. I never really stayed in Jay's room since I had my own. But I remember when we did share a room in school. He liked to keep his things organized in a close manner. The flammable things were spread out so if he made a mistake it wouldn't burn the whole room. He also did that with my stuff even though I hated it.

"We should let him rest," Sam said as she left Jay's side. "God knows what he's going through."

"Right," I started. "I believe we've all had our excitement for today. How about we all meet up later or something for some pizza?"

"Sounds fun," Antoine agreed. "C'mon everyone, let's go." Quickly, the room emptied to leave only Master, Jay and I. Jay was unusually silent so I thought he was sleeping. Master, gazing around the room, was intrigued at intricate doodads of Jay's room. All around the room were items Jay and I found and collected on our adventures. Some things that only he and I knew were from. Master eventually locked his gaze on one particular thing in the room, a picture.

"I don't believe I know who that young lady is in this picture," Master said referring to Fiona. The picture was of Jay, Fiona and I sometime the September before. That was the first picture that us three took together. Each one of us had a copy but Fiona had the original one.

"Oh, that's Fiona," I said. "She was Jay and I's friend."

"Fiona… Fiona…," Master said. "Now where do I know that name from? Ah, I remember. Isn't Fiona a girl you were once sweet on? Unfortunate that she died during Zane's War, is it not?"

"How do you know that?" I asked.

"Richard," Master turned to me. "I know your history. It is no secret most of the things you do. I know because it is my job as your teacher to know. But, I do understand that some things must be kept private. With that, her death is no secret - "

"And I don't want it to be," I cut in.

"It is no secret because the whole world saw her die," Master continued. "Most do not know her name or what she was to you but they saw with their own eyes her fate."

"You must don't know her fate, Master," Jay croaked. "Because she's still inside Rick and I."

"I understand," was all Master could mumble. Looking at both Jay and I, he left the room in silence. His footsteps were heavy against the wood floor so we knew when he left. Even after the creek of the wood ended, Jay and I were still in silence for a while. I knew Jay was watching me but I kept my stare at the picture on the wall. After a while I felt something in the corner of my eye.

"I know you miss her," Jay broke the silence. "Because I miss her too, Rick. The difference is that I can believe it and you can't. You want her here no matter what. I know, it's because you loved her. You still do."

"Does she talk to you?" I swallowed hard.

"What?" Jay asked.

"Does she talk to you, Jay?" I almost yelled.

"No," he said simply. "I can't talk to dead people."

"Then you will never know how I feel." I turned to him with red, wet eyes. "No one does."

"Dude," Jay started. The symbol on my hand began to stir. Jay's emotions then began to pour into my consciousness. Sadness, sorrow, grief, no happiness. Then I let him feel how I felt. As our minds connected, no happiness was found. Only remorse for each other was passed to one another. But once, I felt it. Two bits of our sadness collided and it created hope. Hope that one day we would be happy even though the state of the world around us. "I'm right here with you, I always have been."

"Best friends for eternity, right?" I asked.

"You bet," he answered. "I'm fine, go rest up and tell the others tomorrow."

"Are you sure?"

"Yeah."

"Okay," Fiona and I said slowly. I felt her presence as I left the room. She had a feeling of warmth and joy surrounding her being. She tried to wash away all of the bad feeling I had but a few stayed. The headache that she gave me this time was intense. Pain surged my brain as I plopped down in my bed. Then slowly, painfully, I fell asleep.

CHAPTER VII

The Cursed Stone

Monday, July 30th, 2068. There was someone in my room. I could tell even with my eyes closed. Straining my muscles, I slowly turned over in my bed. Brooke was next to my nightstand holding onto some meat lovers' pizza. I was surprised that I didn't smell it but I was kinda disoriented.

"Well, good afternoon, sunshine." Brooke said as she set the pizza down.

"Afternoon?" I asked

"Yeah," she began. "You missed the little outing you planned so I came to check on you."

"I shouldn't be the one to check on," I stated. "I'm fine, you should go check on Jay."

"I did already," she said as she sat on the end of my bed. "He's asleep right now but when I came he was awake. He told me he was in pain. The pain isn't that bad so it'll be over in a few days." Then, lowering her back, she laid down on my bed sideways with her face towards mine.

Realizing that I was only wearing boxers and a t-shirt, I felt embarrassed. I rarely get embarrassed. I scooted over and patted the empty spot on the bed I had made. Quickly, Brooke slid over to the side of me. Staring at her, I became shy. Her brown eyes went great with her brown, flowing hair. Somehow, I was being pulled towards her.

I don't know how to explain it. Someone help me out here. I was still staring at her. I didn't know what to do. I wasn't that great with girls. I just stared. Then, my hand slowly began to touch her flawless face. I leaned in closer. Closer. Suddenly, our faces met each other and we kissed. Not noticing what I was doing, I pulled my face back and stared at her again.

"What was that for?" she smiled.

"Just trying something," I said unsure. "Did I make you feel uncomfortable?"

"Not at all," she continued to smile. Then she stood, and headed towards the door. "We both have busy schedules today. I left yours along with the pizza. I'll meet up with you later, Rick." Then, like that, she was gone.

I finished off the pizza slowly to savor the entire flavor. On the side of the empty plate was the note Brooke left me. Mostly it was little chores I had to do around the island. The three main things I had to do; talk to my parents, talk to Chris, and finally, meet up with Master and the rest of my friends (excluding Jay, of course). The tasks seemed simple enough so I put on my gear, checked on Jay and headed out.

First, I had to speak to my parents. The time since they found out that I was a Guardian, I have to keep them updated on things since they're not out there in the action. They probably knew about the attack at the conference already but I like to share with them my experiences hands on. Other than Headmaster Ravenhawl and I, they stay out of the way of other Guardians.

"Son, long time no see!" My father greeted me as I stepped through their door.

"Well, yeah," I sat down on the couch. "I've been busy… saving the world and stuff, you know?"

"No excuses," my mom said as she walked in with chocolate milk and Rick. Let me explain, yeah, there's another guy I know named Rick. He looks about thirty and he was the transportation for the school. I never saw him around that much nor did I know a lot about him. Actually, I only talked to him twice beforehand. Once, when I first was arriving to school, and again when we had to move to Bikini Atoll.

"Hey, Rick." I said. "I don't see you around that much."

"I go where I'm needed," he responded.

"Stop pestering our guests, Rick," my mother said as she sat down. "Now, tell us, what have you been up to this past week?" Recalling all of my adventures up to then, I had them on the edges of their seats. Rick seemed unaffected as if he knew all the twists and turns of my epic tale. As my story came to a conclusion, my parents and Rick applauded my bravery as they always did.

"I'm proud of you, son." My father said proudly. "Everyone should be."

"I'm just doing my job," I smiled.

We talked for a little bit more about unimportant things. Just small talk. I missed my parents and they missed me. I wished they could go on adventures with me and help me with things. That would be cool, wouldn't it? It kinda sucked that my parents weren't superheroes but then again, they were in less danger than I was and I was okay with that.

"I appreciate you guys listen to me ramble," I said as I stood. "Well, I guess I'll go now, I have other things to attend to."

"Bye, son," my mom said. "Be careful."

"I'll try," I really would.

I was about halfway out the door when the other Rick called me.

"Rick," the other Rick said.

"Hunh?" I asked.

"Be careful out there, a lot of people are counting on you," he said.

"Will do," I nodded and left out the door.

Chris's garage wasn't that far from my parents house. The buzz of mechanical noises pierced my ears when I got in range of the garage. Chris, Millicent and a few Guardians worked here to fix broken devices and technical things for the rest of us that were illiterate of the subject.

"Hey, Chris," I said as I found him in the garage. "You wanted to see me?"

"Actually, I did," Chris then sat down something he was working on and stood. "Follow me." Walking though all the broken pieces on the floor, I took in all of the scenery. I got a few nods from the other Guardians as we passed through most of the shop. The good thing about Guardian engineers was that they could weld magic into their creations, making them better. Even without magic, Chris was a good builder.

"Welcome, to my super secret project!" Chris exclaimed as he brought me to a giant room. There were ten covered up objects scattered across the room. Millicent was in the far corner and I waved to her, giving her a big grin.

"What exactly is your super secret project?" I asked.

"I'm about to show you," he responded. "That's why I wanted to see you, I'm finally done."

"I hope you took breaks," I said. "I wouldn't want you cooped up in this place all day."

"Nah," he said. "Millicent and I go out sometimes to enjoy the waves. But I do miss Baton Rouge. I just miss being in a big city."

"Me too," I admitted. "But we can't dwindle on the past, man. We gotta live in the moment."

"Yeah, that's exactly why I've been working so hard on this project," he pointed to the covered up items. "They remind me of the city."

"Hm, I wonder what it is…" I pondered.

"I'll show you," Chris said happily. Then he walked me over to the closest one. "Behold!" He said when he uncovered the object. Completely shocked, my eyes widened. A brand new, black motorcycle stood before me. It had a lightning emblem on each side that stood out from the black. The helmet was black also, with a black visor to give it an astonishing look.

"Uh, Chris," I said.

"Yeah?" he asked. "It's amazing right?"

"It would be even more amazing if I could drive it," I said dryly. "I haven't gotten my driver's license."

"Who's gonna pull you over when you're going at lightning speed chasing bad guys?" Chris started. "I'm pretty sure you don't need a driver's license to drive this thing where you're going. C'mon get on it, try it."

"Not right now," I said. "Maybe later. I have other places to go now. Are the rest of them motorcycles too?"

"Yeah," he confirmed. "One for each of your friends."

"Well, thanks, Chris," I said. "I'll be sure to tell them. Can you keep them in here when we're not using them? You're right, they might come in handy one day."

"Sure do, Ricky. Haha." he laughed. "Well you and me have busy schedules today, it'll be best if I head back to my work."

"So will I," I said shaking his hand. Chris and I said our farewells and I headed to the Commons Area in the center of Bikini Island.

The group was already there waiting on me, so I quickly grabbed a seat in the group. Master was giving me a stern look as if I needed to be chastised. Then, I noticed that Jay was there too, barely awake but he was there. Jay and the rest of the group were clearly waiting on me to talk, something important.

"Did I miss anything?" I asked.

"Yes, you did, Richard," Master said. "Jay, would you like to explain?"

From where he sat, Jay then rustled in his seat. Once he was comfortable, he spoke. "Um, it's about something I overheard Maggie say," he mumbled. "Tell him, Rick, what she said."

"What?" I was confused. "She didn't say-"

"Tell him, Rick," Jay said. "We can't waste time."

Recollecting my thoughts, I tried to remember what Maggie was saying to me. It was so long ago that I had put it in the back of my mind so it was fuzzy. "What is it you're looking for?" I asked Master.

"Rick," Jay started. "The Crystal of Life."

Oh, I remembered. Maggie thought I knew where it was. Honestly, I had never heard of such thing until she uttered it. But it was still hard to remember what she said.

"She thought I knew where it was," I started. "Like, she really thought I knew where it was."

"Did she give any locations?" Master asked. "Anything important, tell me."

"No," I shook my head. "Nothing."

Master then leaned in close to the whole group. "Do you know what The Crystal of Life is?"

Master's question was followed by silence. I was pretty sure if I hadn't heard of it then they didn't hear of it either.

"The Crystal of Life is a powerful object, an ancient myth," Master began. "It is said that it was created long before creatures and humans arrived on this planet but is only sought by humans. Legend has it that whoever stains their blood on the Crystal shall live forever. Not only that, it can bring back the dead from their eternal sleep. But, of course, this is only a legend. Legends are usually thought of to be false…but Zane's followers think otherwise."

"If there is such a thing then someone should have found it by now." Sam said.

"There are many claims of someone finding the Cursed Stone," Master said. "Battles have been fought over it, the legend."

"Why did you call it the Cursed Stone?" Dane asked. "Shouldn't it be the opposite?"

"Oh, no," Master answered. "So many have died to find the thing and there's even a legend that says it does the opposite; once you touch it, you die. That would explain all of the disappearances of the Guardians who go after it."

"But what would Maggie want with it?" I asked.

"What does everyone else want?" Master retaliated. "To live forever!"

"So, what, do you believe that this Crystal actually exists?" I asked.

"I am skeptical," he explained. "But if the one you call Maggie gets her hands on this it will be worse than Zane's War."

"Well we have to stop her!" Lance butted in. "We can't just sit here and do nothing."

"Correct," Master answered. "That is why I am sending a few of you to investigate." The crowd became quiet. There were ten of us, clearly he had plenty to choose from. "I hate to say this but Rick, you're going."

"Great," I said instantly. I looked around, "I only want Jay to come with me."

"He can go but you need more with you," he said.

"Fine," I thought for a second. "Antoine and Sam."

"I would prefer you had a Guardian of each element," Master said. "Now you need a water and Earth Guardian."

"I'll go!" Brooke butted in. "I want to go…"

"No-" I was interrupted.

"Well, two wind Guardians should suffice for one Earth. Perfect!" exclaimed Master. "The rest of you can stay here and train and help around the island. You five should be able to leave out tomorrow."

"What exactly are we suppose to be doing?" Jay asked.

"Oh, it's simple enough," Master said as he stood. "You are to find Maggie and find out where the stone is."

"So, you're sending five teenagers to look for a myth?" Jay questioned. "Sounds safe."

"You've been through worse, haven't you?" He laughed. "Do you not believe in yourself?"

"I don't believe in the Crystal," he said. "I don't like pointless missions."

"You don't have to go," I said. "You're still kinda hurt."

That ticked him off. "Are you saying that I'm weak?" he said angrily.

"Weak," I agreed.

"Screw it, I'm going," He told Master.

"If you really were serious you would already be packing," Master said. "The enemy doesn't wait on us. I would go with you but I am too fragile. And I think teenagers work best when they are unsupervised in some situations."

"Don't worry," I said. "I'll get the job done."

"I believe in you," He said. "I believe in all of you."

Then he turned his back to us, drowning out his face in the sunset.

CHAPTER VIII

Birthday, It's Yah Birthday

Monday, August 6, 2068. I groaned as I pushed away the millionth overgrown leaf out of my path. The crunches of the wet leaves under my boots were rhythmic as if I was listening to a catchy song. Four other pairs of magical footwear followed behind me, making more music. Listening carefully to our footsteps, one of the pair of boots became offbeat.

"Ouch," Brooke moaned after she fell to the ground. Remember, ladies, the best way to gain attention is to fall on the ground and pretend to be hurt. Three boys will notice, trust me. I turned around to see Brooke laying her cute butt on the jungle floor waiting for someone to pick her up. Antoine stretched out his hand to Brooke and she struggled to grab it. Antoine hoisted Brooke off the ground and she dusted herself off.

"Have you ever heard of watching your feet, girlie?" Sam asked as we continued on our voyage into the green sea.

"I tripped on a tree root. I'm not used to this," She responded.

"Well, we're not exactly in Georgia anymore, B. The jungles of South America don't have southern hospitality." Antoine pointed out. "Trust me, this place creeps me out too."

Only one week ago. One week since we left Bikini Atoll and we only had one lead to The Crystal. When we arrived in California we had no idea where we were going or how we were getting there. Of course, you can meet anyone in Cali and we so happened to meet someone who was helpful to us.

The firefighter we begged to help us pointed us to an artifacts museum a few blocks away. We were lucky enough to not be noticed by anyone in the town. Well, we were five, noticeable, unsupervised teens wearing all black combat clothes. Californians tend to not notice weird things so we were all good.

Once we arrived in the museum, we searched for anything that could lead us to Maggie. We had to find out what she was after. The Cursed Stone was primarily sought out by humans so there had to be something about it in human possession.

"Hmm, The Lover's Stone, Rolling Stones, kidney stones," Sam said as she flipped through the museum pamphlet. "Nothing on the Cursed Stone."

"Keep searching." I said. "We have literally nowhere else to go. Our mission is to find our target. If we don't, then we've failed Master."

"Your speeches are so dumb, dude." Jay said nonchalantly as he waded around the area we were in. I know I talk a lot but I talk with a reason. Sometimes the things he says are just pointless, stupid ... and dumb. Just like what he told me. Being ignorant, I had to respond to his comment.

"These 'speeches' are better than some of the crap you say." I laughed to Jay. "Do you need some more toilet paper, bro?"

"Oh, you're a comedian now." Jay said sarcastically. "How about you show me your moves? Right here, right now."

Jay and I got into fighting position right in that room. I honestly did not want to fight him but I had to claim my dominance. He had been picking on me the whole trip to Cali and I didn't want the rest of the gang to think I was weak. Weakness cannot lead a group. If weakness lead a group then the whole group becomes weak. The weak get killed and I didn't want anyone to die.

"Guys, stop." Antoine said. "Look at this." Antoine was pointing at a painting on the wall. The four of us hurried over to Antoine to get a closer look. I had not forgotten about Jay that easily and I smacked him on the back of his head when he least expected it. Jay gave me a long snarl and focused his attention towards the canvas.

The first drawing was of a man holding a stone. The stone was small, small enough to fit in the man's hand. The second drawing showed the man with the stone surrounded by what looked like his family. Two small figures and another adult sized one next to the man. The man was protecting the stone from his family, secluding it from the group.

The third drawing was of two adult figures, the man with the stone and a somewhat hunch backed figure. Again, the man was protecting the other figures from the stone. I guessed that the older one was his wife and the other two adult figures were his children. The fourth drawing now only had three figures. Two were hunched over and appeared to have beards of some sort. The man with the stone was there again protecting the stone against the elders. The man with the stone hadn't changed since the second drawing.

The final picture only had one figure. The man with the stone stood alone with the rock above his head just like the first picture.

"Well, that guy must be lonely." I said after everyone had looked at the last picture. "You guys think it's the Cursed Stone?"

"Like you said, we have no other lead. Might as well check this one out." Sam said as she read the info card under the paintings.

"'This painting was found in the deep jungles of South America. It is believed that this painting is from an ancient civilization that lived in the vicinity. Researchers have not found any evidence to what the painting is about or what it stands for. No research has been conducted since its finding in 1864.'" Sam read.

"Oh, God." Brooke whispered. "Don't tell me have to go to South America, Rick."

"I'm afraid we have to," I sighed. "It's the only lead we have."

From there we snuck our way around the *Estados Unidos* and made our way to South America. And no, South America is not like the South in the U.S. It is a completely different atmosphere. Like, literally, only 1/1,000,000 of the people spoke fluent English so I had to get direction to the right jungle from a Google Map. The thing had cost me $20 and I could barely work it. I had to get Brooke to show me how to slide my fingers across the holographic to make the map larger and pinch my fingers together to make it smaller.

So there we were. I was about to start singing to myself soon. ♪*In the jungle, the mighty jungle, the lion sleeps tonight*♪. That's from a song that came out when my grandfather wasn't even born. I assumed so; I had never even met my grandfather.

"Let's take a break," I said. "It's getting dark." We found a clear spot to settle down in for the night in no time. While the rest of them set up their tents, I went to go start a fire. Half of the job was already done considering I can set things on fire with my hands but I had to gather firewood. Since everyone else was busy I went by myself.

Returning from my adventure I noticed that my group had set up tents around where the soon to be fire would be. I dropped the sticks into a pile and created a set of embers with my Guardian powers.

"So, who packed marshmallows?" Brooke asked as I sat down.

"Right here!" Antoine exclaimed. He then grabbed a bag from behind the log he was sitting on. As he passed the bag around, he began to speak again. "I saved them for story time."

"Story time?" Jay questioned.

"Yeah," Antoine answered. "Every campfire needs a story. I assume I'm the best storyteller here so I'll take the lead."

"Shouldn't we be getting some rest? We have to-" I began to say.

"Shut up, dude." Antoine said. "No disrespect. Now, where do I begin? Hmm, well…" He stuffed a marshmallow in his mouth and swallowed it whole. "When I was a little kid my mom always told me there were scary creatures. I didn't believe her at first…then I met Brooke."

"Heyyy," Brooke dragged out sadly, as we all laughed.

"But I know of something even creepier than Brooke. It's a creature made of pure darkness. It was created from the sad dreams of humans and Pomegas. My mom told me that if anyone ever met this creature they would be haunted forever. They would never have good luck ever again and have horrible nightmares at least once a month."

"Sounds spooky," I said sarcastically. "Too bad I've already had enough of curses and ancient myths for a lifetime." I latched onto the log and hoisted myself up.

"Nope, you sit down right there." Jay said. "You're not going anywhere."

"Hey," I frowned. "You don't tell me what to do."

"Fine then," Jay looked at me. "Leave."

Right then, I realized that Jay was trying to take over my leadership. The leadership I had gained. It seemed that the encounter with the fairy did not change my best friend's mindset about me. I had to end that. It was too late that night because Jay had already defeated me verbally. Slowly, I glared at Jay as I sat down.

"Now where was I?" Antoine started again. "Right, the poor souls who encounter this creature are called The Disturbed because their lives are, well, disturbed. Some say that The Disturbed are loyal

71

to the thing and do its will. There is no way to beat it so there are no survivors to tell the tale. No one even knows how it looks. But I'm pretty sure it's ugly because why else would they call it…a Nightmare. That's where humans get the saying from."

"Well I can believe it." Sam said. "I've heard weirder stuff in the past week."

"We all have and we don't need to hear Guardian myths when we need to be resting." I said.

"Aren't we going after a myth?" Antoine said. "If the Crystal of Life is out there then for sure The Nightmare is lurking somewhere."

"Yeah, yeah. I think that did it. I'm going to bed," I said as I stood up. "We're leaving at seven, be ready." I started walking to my tent.

Hm, I thought to myself. The only reason I didn't believe in Antoine's Nightmare story is because my worst nightmare had already came true. I had lost Fiona. And, even worse, she was talking to me. That made me want her even more. It made me reach for something I knew I couldn't grasp.

I snuggled down in my sleeping bag and covered my face to block the mosquitoes. I kinda looked forward to talking to Fiona but she must have been asleep herself. Well, that is if spirits or whatever she is sleep. Maybe she was a ghost forever haunting me because she sacrificed herself for me. I know for sure I missed her though.

I heard the group laugh at one of Antoine's stupid jokes. I chose to be alone. I could've went out there but it wasn't for me. I had to strategize. I had to plan. I had to-

"Hey, can I come in?" I heard Brooke's muffled voice outside of my tent.

"Sure," I said and she let herself in. Brooke had her hair in a bun with her pajamas on. With her, she carried some Meat Lovers' Pizza and two drinks. I scooted over and she plopped down next to me with a soft thump.

"What's the occasion?" I asked as I stared back and forth at Brooke and the pizza. I'm sorry, it would be a very hard choice for me to choose between a beautiful, bodacious brunette or delicious, warm Meat Lovers' Pizza.

"Oh, you know," she looked at me. "It's just my sixteenth birthday. Sweet sixteen, haha."

"Oh, um, happy birthday," I stuttered. "I don't have a present for you. You should've told me earlier."

"It's fine," Brooke laughed. "I know you're busy. It's just a date. It's not that important."

"Just a date?" I questioned. "Brooke, it's your sweet sixteen. It's suppose to be one of the best days of your life. Spending all of your birthday in the woods. Some sweet sixteen you're having, haha."

"Yeah, well, you know, saving the world is more important than my birthday." She said as she handed me some food. "But at least I'm with you."

I laughed, shocked. "Wow, thanks Brooke. I didn't know I was that important to you. I'm glad I made your birthday better."

She snuggled up closer to me. "You made it fantastic." Then, her face was inches from mine. I could smell her perfume.

73

Strawberries. Mm, strawberries. Her kiss was soft and gentle. That's where the scent had came from. She had planned to do this. That's why girls wear lip-gloss, right? It felt the same as when she did it the first time. But that time it just didn't feel right. She didn't feel right. I didn't feel right.

Fiona wouldn't like this.

"Brooke," I whispered. "You know about Fiona, don't you?"

Brooke caught me in her gaze and replied softly, "She's dead, I'm not." She then realized her mistake and added an extra remark. "Five months of sadness won't bring her back."

"I know," I said. "You don't understand."

"What do you mean I don't understand?" she said. "It's simple-"

"It's not simple, okay?" I yelled.

She stared at me.

"No, look, Brooke, I'm sorry, okay?" I grabbed her arm.

Quiet as a mouse, she escaped my grasp, left my side, and began to leave my tent. "Just remember who's here for you," she said as she left me to be alone in my tent.

"But Fiona was there for me," I whispered to myself. "She saved my life. In more ways than I can imagine."

CHAPTER IX

You Ruin My Life

Tuesday, August 7, 2068. Four, long, sweaty hours of traveling and we finally stumbled upon what we thought was our destination. Brooke was last in our little trail because she probably still didn't like me from last night. Oh, well. She would get over it. Antoine and Jay were betting on who would find the Crystal first and Jay thought he had a pretty good clue what to look for. I, on the other foot, thought that I would find the Crystal first with my lightning powers and take all of the glory.

The ruin was a giant hole in the ground. Literally, it went twenty feet straight in the Earth. I jumped down first to make sure it was safe and the rest followed. Jay and I lit our hands with fire to create some light so everyone could see. After about thirty seconds of searching along the wall, Sam brushed upon what substituted as a door.

"Hey, I found something!" she yelled.

"What is it?" I asked.

"I think it's our way in," she replied.

"Well, ladies first," Antoine chuckled.

"Jerk," Brooke said as she pushed Antoine out of the way. Sam shoved the stone door with all of her might but the door was, well, a stone door. Brooke added her strength along with Sam's and the door still didn't budge. "Crap," was the nice way of putting what Sam said.

"I'm the only Earth Guardian here," I said stepping up. "Let me try." The girls moved out of the way as I placed my hands on the cold stone. Rooting my feet to the ground, I grew Earth boots around my feet to keep them in place. Then, with a mighty heave, I slid the massive door out of the doorway.

De-rooting myself from the ground, I stepped into the cool, dark ruins with my fireball trailing behind. With my Guardian eyes, I scanned the room as the others piled in. There were four doorways in the room including the entrance. In the middle of the dark room, there stood a giant stone statue gave the entire room a creepy feeling.

Sprouting from the back of the stone creature were eight long tentacles. Its slender body only mounted one eye that covered half of what I thought was its face. The bottom half of its "face" was covered with a mouth full of sharp teeth that would give the Pomega a run for its money. Skinny arms and legs extended from its body and ended with razor sharp claws that would make the pyramids jealous.

"What the heck is that thing?" Jay asked, being drawn toward the massive statue. "Looks like Rick when he gets angry."

"Looks more like your mom," I replied. "I think it'll be best if no one touches it. That thing's creepy." As I said that, I was also drawn towards Jay's mom and knelt down at the base of the statue. I moved the fireball closer to illuminate the engraving on the stone and tried to comprehend the writing. After scanning the first row of symbols I gave up.

"Just our luck," I sighed. "It's not in English."

"I think this place is way older than English," Antoine butted in. He then quickly glanced around the room. "Waay older."

The fear in Antoine's voice put me on the edge. Usually, Antoine is full of courage and all the other stuff that the lion from *The Wizard of Oz* lacked. But Antoine wasn't looking really liony right then. I went over, patted Antoine on the shoulder, and looked at the three doorways in front of us.

"Sam, which door do you think we should go through?" I asked politely.

"Hmm," she hesitated. "Eenie, meanie, minie, mo." She pointed at the one on the left.

Everyone stood and stared at the doorway. "Well, let's go, people. The Crystal isn't gonna find itself." I said as I headed for the darkness. I didn't hear footsteps behind me and I shouted a few more words of encouragement.

"C'mon guys, It's not that ba-" I was going to say "bad" but the screech of bats cut off my sentence. The black creatures swarmed over me right as I stepped in the darkness of the doorway. I tried to protect my face as well as could. But you all know me. I'm so clumsy that I stumbled to the ground. Eventually, the bats either scattered around the room or went down the other two hallways.

"You had to pick the creepiest one?" Jay asked sarcastically as he walked forward into the hallway. "It was kinda funny seeing Rick fall, though." I heard his voice echo in the hallway.

I was second in the hallway after I picked myself up. Antoine and the girls stayed close behind me. "No splitting up, this isn't Scooby-Doo." I guess you can already tell that I like retro stuff. The early two thousands were way more fascinating than our time. There is not that much creativity since computers do everything for us. Can you believe that home computers only held gigabytes?

"Great, another room," Jay sighed as the hallway ended.

As the rest of us piled in, Jay and I increased our fireballs to spread light to the entire room. "I told you you picked the creepiest one." Jay said as we surveyed the chamber. Coffins, coffins everywhere. Every nook and cranny was filled with them. Some huge, some small enough for dogs. There had to be about four hundred in there.

"Eww," Brooke cringed. "What sick person did this?"

"The last people to come here were archeologists. And I don't think they had a motive to use any of these." I said. Even though they are in the business of bones.

"You think the Crystal's in here?" Jay asked to no one in particular.

"I don't think life and death fit well in the same room," Sam reasoned. "Looks like we have to go deeper into the ruin."

"We should search these first," I said.

"No way, I'm going in any of these things," Brooke shrieked.

"Pssft, you're no help," Antoine sighed. "We should've brought Lance instead of you. I'm not scared to get my hands dirty. Lay it on me!" He said all of this as he swaggered to the nearest coffin and plopped it opened.

Antoine screamed as spiders poured out of the black box of death. I laughed as he tried to brush them all away with wind as he bounced around the room trying not to touch any of them. "Not cool, man." He said as he flicked the last spider away with his finger.

"That's what you get for being all cocky," I laughed. "At least we know now that the Crystal isn't in here."

"Let's go," Sam urged. "The sooner we get out of here, the better."

She was right. I was ready to leave myself but I was so determined to get the mission completed. We walked through several more rooms full of blood, torture devices, more coffins, and occasionally, empty rooms. As we tried to search each area, the entrance to the ruins became further and further away and it made me feel trapped. Maybe we wouldn't find our way out even if we did find the Crystal.

"Now look at this big mama," Jay exclaimed as we entered another room. The "big mama" was a large stone coffin built into the ground in the middle of the room. Around the coffin, the symbols that I saw on the statue were engraved all around the thing with even more definition. Like 2160p.

79

"This must be where the Crystal is," Antoine said. "I mean, look at it. They wouldn't put it in the middle of the room all loud and proud if it wasn't important."

Brooke tried to reach out and touch it. "No, not yet," I warned. I don't know how I knew, but I knew it wasn't safe. I cleared my mind and tried to reach inside the coffin. Penetrating the stone was the hard part, what was inside was the weird part. A mix of ancient and evil powers laid inside the stone. Almighty and powerful, it emitted power beyond my comprehension. Quickly, I backed out of the coffin as to not get trapped inside the ancient knowledge.

"The Crystal is defiantly in there," I said.

"Wonderful, then you just made our work way easier," a hushed shadow laughed.

My entire group turned around towards the familiar voice. Where the sound had came from, there was nothing but darkness. I did a double take of the room and made sure none of the girls had said that.

"Over here, idiot."

Maggie then detached herself from the shadows and revealed her cruel beauty. "Thanks, sis," she said as she plopped down on her knees. Her sister, Elisa, slowly crept down the wall in her shadow form with a huge smile on her face.

"What are you two doing here?" I asked.

"Same reason you are," she then jokingly pointed at the coffin. "Seems as if that thing is in high demand this time of the year."

"Why do you even want it?" Brooke asked trying to be brave.

"Why do you even want it?" Maggie mimicked annoyingly. "Why would anyone want it? To control life and death, that's why. The Shadow doesn't fool with petty stuff. And I classify you, you, you, you, and you as petty. Now if you will just-"

"What is The Shadow?" I asked.

"Hm, I'm glad you asked," Maggie's lips reached up to her eyes. "I'd like to introduce you to," she pointed toward the dark hallway on the side of her. "The Shadow." Slowly, Seth crept out of the shadows all healed up and stuff. Cracking his knuckles, his facial expression became solid as a rock.

Jay laughed, "You're joking, right?" He asked. I swear I saw him wipe a tear of joy from his eye.

"No, we're quite serious," Elisa hissed for the first time. From behind Seth appeared my best bud, Lunk. I hadn't seen Lunk since the day I killed Zane. He looked exactly the same. Compared to Seth, though, he appeared to be a regular sized man but with extruding muscles. The two living Hulks moved further into the room as the fake Guardians from New York marched behind them.

"Two emo chicks, Arnold Schwarzenegger, Rambo and a bunch of imitation Guardians," Sam counted. "So far the only thing scary about you guys is the name. And it's not even that great." I laughed to myself. Sam, she was always a trooper.

"Let's see what you got then, girlie," Maggie taunted as she got into fighting position. "Usually the ones that talk a lot have nothing to back it up."

81

Everyone stared at me for instructions. "Just be careful," I said to everyone. "Remember, our main goal is to get the Crystal and get out of here. If beating these guys is part of it then I can't stop you from having fun." They all nodded as if saying "Right," and we all got into fighting position. I already knew Sam was headed for Maggie so I aimed my sights on Elisa.

Sprinting forward, I remembered the first time I had fought Elisa. She would use her shadow form to easily get away. The only way I beat her last time was to get her to transform back into her slick, human figure. Knowing this, I flew into the air aiming for Elisa's head.

She sidestepped and dodged my attack. As predicted, she turned into her shadow form and crawled onto the wall. I clawed out, grabbed for her, and latched on as hard as I could. I tried with all of my might not to merge with her so I kept my face far away from her figure as we flew up on the wall.

My punches landed on her body one after the other making her stumble a little every time. Her shadow form was not an element so it didn't have a weakness that I knew of. But I had an element that no one else alive had, lightning. I reached down, grabbed the dagger on my side, and launched it into the shadow with brute force.

Elisa screamed when the metal pierced her. She did not change back to her human form so I released some of the electricity stored inside the dagger.

My hands grasped onto her squishy stomach as she turned back into a human. Then I realized that we were flying in the air.

Were.

As we descended hard towards the stone ground, I tried to pull myself so that my feet would hit the ground first. I let go of Elisa and I began descend at my own pace. Landing softly on my feet, I turned to face Elisa again, who was already launching toward me.

I blocked her hit as I ducked under and tried to stab her again. What, if a chick was trying to kill you you wouldn't be thinking about being a gentleman either. You know, I hate that stereotype so much. Girls always want to be equal but I not suppose to treat them certain ways. I mean, I do it. I would consider myself a gentleman. I'm gentle with the ladies. Right? Right?

Unfortunately, my stab attack missed and I had to quickly sheath my weapon. Going under her legs, I turned around in mid air and pushed her in her back with rock hands. As my enemy fell to the ground, I seized the opportunity to glance around the room.

Sam was in hand-to-hand combat with Maggie still. Antoine and Jay took on Seth and Lunk and Brooke was fighting three imitation Guardians by herself. I felt as if I needed to help her but I knew she could hold her own. I had a personal problem I had to take care of myself, anyway.

"You're weaker than you were last time," I said proudly. "Or I just got stronger."

"If anything, you got more annoying," she hissed.

"That's weird because a lot of girls say that," I realized. "You're not the first…or won't be the last."

"I'm guessing you're not very good with the ladies," she laughed as she got to her feet. I was going to give a smart reply back but Elisa grabbed me around my stomach and rammed me into a wall. I coughed up a little blood and became dizzy.

Despite my dizziness, Elisa turned back into her shadow form and hauled me into the air. Again, I tried to keep my face as far away from her as I could. This time, though, I was caught off guard so I had less time to react. My hands weren't fast enough to block my face from being sucked into hers. I screamed as half of my face got converted into that shadow stuff.

I used all of my strength to try to pull my face away from Elisa. Every few tries I would get my face a reasonable amount away from her but it felt as if I was stitched to her then. No matter how hard I tried I was trapped flying in the air with a half shadowy face.

"I learned from last time," she laughed as she knocked my body into the ceiling. "You can't get away so easily." She cackled.

"Well, I do have something you haven't seen in a while." I said, thinking of my next move.

"What is thattt?" she hissed.

"Sunlight," I replied as I lit my entire body on fire. I was satisfied when I heard Elisa curse and then I was suddenly detached from her. My brilliant schemes work best when I'm under pressure, I suppose. But enough of me gloating, I had to get back into the action. I did a back flip in mid-air to look cool even though no one was probably looking at me. I know I wouldn't if I was in a death match.

I blocked Maggie's attack that was intended for Sam as I landed. Maggie punched me in the stomach as I tried to get myself situated on the ground. I was in defense mode as I tried to get in the groove of Maggie's attack pattern. Once that was done, I simply punched her in the stomach to make her stumble back. That gave me enough time to catch my breath.

"Sam," I said catching my breath. "You're good. I can take it from here."

"You're so cocky," Maggie took that time to catch her breath, too. "Actually, too cocky for my liking."

"I have her, Rick," Sam barked from behind me.

Elisa flew over us and transformed out of her shadow form behind Sam. "I think you have more problems, blondie." Elisa said with a crooked smile.

"I hate that word with a freakin' passion," was the last thing Sam said before she turned around and decked Elisa in the face. I heard the girl yell from behind me as I faced Maggie head to head.

"That chick was no threat to me," Maggie said after a long silence. "But you," she glared as she reached behind her for her sword. "I feel as if I have a challenge coming towards me."

As the cold metal from Maggie's sword scraped her sheath, I also drew my sword from its home. Honestly, that was my first time using my sword in real combat. I was kinda nervous going against a master swordsman. But as they said in the early two thousands.... YOLO!

I raced towards Maggie with the point of my sword aimed at her face. I took my first swing and the mighty clash of our swords rang throughout the room. Quickly, I thought, reach back and strike again. Going off of pure adrenaline, I swung my blade for the second time anddddd –

BOOM! A loud crash in the room sent everyone to the ground.

BOOM! Another one.

BOOM! It was coming from the coffin in the middle of the room.

BOOM! "What is that?" Brooke asked.

BOOM! This time the coffin lid came exploding off, leaving rubble. Everyone waited in anticipation. The room was entirely silent making chills run down my spine.

Slowly, anciently, four black claws arose from the coffin and grasped the rim. No, I thought to myself, it can't be.

"It's awake," Elisa almost cried.

CHAPTER X

Sweet Dreams

In my day, I saw some super scary stuff. So far, I had saved the world, survived being starved for almost two months, saw the death of my girlfriend, and talked face to face with a Fire Fairy, but those things on a scale of 1 – 10 were at most a seven. But this…thing had to be a ten million million million million million million million.

Its claws still grasped onto to rim of the coffin as its full body made its journey to the surface. Its other clawed hand reached out and grabbed the rim. Then, from the bowels of its stomach, the creature let out an ear-piercing scream. Everyone covered their ears as the massive black thing flew out of its coffin. Fear kept my eyes locked on the creature as it hovered above all of us.

It was the statue from earlier. Of course, I didn't mean the actual statue. This one was living, breathing, and larger than its statue counterpart. The giant eye at the top of its face was rapidly moving, analyzing all of us. As its eye swept over me I instantly became numb. The only thing I could remember was Fiona's limp body falling to the ground.

"No, it can't be," Antoine shivered. "No," he repeated.

"What is it?" I asked. "Lay it on us."

"It's…it's…" Antoine stalled.

"Say it, dude!" Jay screamed.

"The Nightmare," Antoine cried. "It's real."

It took a second for my brain to register all of that. Alright, let's do one of my favorite things; a checklist:

1. Antoine said that was The Nightmare

2. There is no way to beat The Nightmare

3. People who meet The Nightmare become Disturbed

4. That thing was freakin' ugly

5. There was only one word spinning in my head the entire

    time

"Run!" I shouted as I stumbled to my feet. I headed to what I thought was the exit. I wasn't even going to try to fight that thing. I changed my boots to flee mode and I suddenly began to run faster. Once I was fully out of the corridor I ran down, I stopped in the room to catch my breath.

"Oh, my God," were the first words that escaped my mouth. Do you remember those coffins from earlier? Yeah, well some of them had bodies in them. And those bodies, wait for it, were moving. "Why do these bad things always have to happen to me?" I said to no one. Oh, wait, I realized I was smart enough to bring my sword with me this time. I gripped the hilt of my metal harder for good luck.

"Rick, I'm so glad I found – woah," Jay said as he ran into the room. "I'm guessing these things aren't friendly?" he asked.

"Friendlier than that thing back there," I said sarcastically. The zombies were out of their resting places by now and were surrounding Jay and I. "You ready, bro?"

"I woke up ready," Jay said as he lit his hands on fire. I pressed my back against my best friend as the zombies closed in on us. Then I thought to myself, "What if I just added a little element to the magical steel?" The result was me setting the blade of my sword on fire. Swinging at the nearest zombie, I realized my weapon was a one hit kill. Perfect.

One after the other, I lunged my sword into the stomachs of the zombies, cutting them in half. Jay used fireballs and fire breath to set his enemies in fire, burning them to crisps. Honestly, I thought those things would be more of a challenge. Then again, if something had woken me up from my eternal slumber I would be moving pretty slow too.

"That's the last of them," I said as the last zombie slid from my sword."Where are the others?"

"I don't know," Jay sighed. "After you hightailed it, everyone else scattered. Last thing I saw was Seth and Lunk fighting The Nightmare."

"They're actually fighting that thing?" I laughed. "Maggie has them trained well."

"I'm trained too. But I know when to not pick a fight," Jay said. "Let's find our crew and get out of here."

Brooke screamed off in the distance.

"That didn't sound very good," I said dryly. I waved Jay down as I ran to Brooke's scream. "C'mon, man, let's go."

Right when I stepped into the room Brooke was in, I switched my boots back to combat mode. Brooke was in the room, Elisa, and of course, The Nightmare. Elisa was in some sort of trance hanging in midair before the black beast. Brooke was cringed in the corner watching the whole thing with her eyes spread like butter.

Elisa was in full shadow mode still hanging limply. Suddenly, her shadow stuff slowly crept from her body towards The Nightmare. As Elisa's powers crept towards the Nightmare, the skin under her robe became visible. She was tanner than Maggie and had unhealthy nails. Her hood drew back and revealed her short, black hair that was in curls.

As the last of her shadow powers slithered to The Nightmare, Elisa fell to the ground. The Nightmare roared in triumph, which made Brooke burst into tears. "No," I said as I held Jay back. The Nightmare was not going after Brooke. It was headed for the door on the opposite side of the room. Its tentacles swayed in the air like spaghetti being washed with water. The creature made no noise as it left the room.

"Brooke, are you alright?" Jay asked running to her.

"I'm fine," she said as Jay helped her up. "It was so scary, though."

"I know. It gives everyone the chills," I spoke softly. "What happened?"

"I don't know," she sobbed. "Elisa was chasing after me and that thing appeared out of nowhere. Then, Elisa spoke in some weird tongue to it and she got lifted into the air. That's when I screamed and you guys came in."

"Tounge?" Jay asked. "I didn't know Elisa knew other languages."

"It wasn't words," Brooke corrected. "It was like hisses and snarls. Like an animal."

"Never heard of that one before," Jay said. "You?" he asked me.

"No," I said sadly. "Elisa's not our problem, though. We need to find Sam and Antoine-"

"C'mon, you wind freak," Maggie roared from the hallway. Sam was being backed into the room by Maggie's sword. Sam had her arm shield deployed as the metal continued to send her backwards. Every once in a while Sam would try to hit her but Maggie was too quick for her. Sam's shield could only bear so much before it began to dent and she was forced to retreat.

Sam stumbled backwards on Elisa's body and fell to her butt. Maggie grinned because she knew that the fight was over. The grin didn't last long, through, because Maggie soon realized what Sam had tripped over.

91

"Elisa!" Maggie screamed in fear. Maggie ran and shoved a dazed Sam out of the way to reach Elisa. Maggie placed her ear to Elisa and listened for a heartbeat.

Silence.

"She's alive," she sighed. Then, in one quick movement, Maggie flashed her eyes around the room and spotted us. Then she flashed to Sam. Then to Elisa. "Who did this?"

"The Nightmare," I said boldly. "She was like that when we got here."

Slowly, she grabbed Elisa and hoisted her as she stood up. "I hate all of you, but which way did it go?" Jay pointed to where the monster had made its grand exit. "I'm going to go kill that thing. Then, I'm coming back for all of you." Maggie took her time as she walked to her doom with The Nightmare.

"Sam, are you alright?" I asked.

Sam stirred on the ground for a bit. "Yeah, I'm good," she said, out of breath. "Just a couple of scratches, ya know? And my butt, ow, that hurts."

"We should get butt guards installed," I joked. "Seems like a good investment."

Jay and I went to go help Sam onto her feet. Sam was almost as tall as I was. Her blonde hair was regular length with pink highlights. Dane had given her a necklace with the letter 'S' on it. Her fiery spirit was still strong in her even though she was almost killed. That's what I liked about Sam, she was a fighter and a trooper.

"Let's find Antoine and get out of here," Jay said. "This ruin is getting crazier by the minute."

Jay said it. I was ready to go back to Bikini Atoll. Forget about the Crystal of Life. Forget about The Nightmare. Forget about Maggie. But we needed to find Antoine and the exit without becoming Disturbed. Being Disturbed was the least of my worries since I had encountered the thing twice and I hadn't changed yet.

So, we were lost in the ruins and we were missing a team member. Let me just say that it wasn't my fault that something bad always happens to the people that hang with me. Like that time when we went to go calm down the Loch Ness Monster. Yeah, it exists. It's one of the only creatures that humans can naturally see so Guardians have to keep it under constant surveillance. I took my squad and Squad B to see it and Lance ends up almost being the things dinner. But, yeah, this whole Nightmare thing is another example.

The four of us made our way around the labyrinth for a good thirty minutes. Along the way, we met our good friends, the zombies, who according to Sam were the undead Disturbed. The Nightmare must have figured that it didn't need to call the real Disturbed to fight us. But who cares, it made it easier for us to get the heck out of there. Mike Tyson would be jealous of how fast we were killing those things.

Finally, we got to some entertaining action. Maggs and Antoine were, get this, ARGUEING over who would FIGHT The Nightmare. Seth and Lunk were just as confused as I was while the giant monster thing was kept busy by the imitation Guardians. Antoine isn't crazy, but that had crossed the line.

"No, it's mine," Maggie argued. "I don't care what your mammy said."

"This thing has been my worst nightmare since I was a little kid," Antoine yelled. "I deserve to kill it."

"It almost killed my sister!"

"Anyone can kill your sister!"

"Hey," I interrupted. "Are you people crazy?" Instantly, I knew that was a big mistake. I then shook my hands in front of my face. "But you guys can argue about cheese if you wanna."

Suddenly, The Nightmare swiped away all of the imitation Guardians with its tentacles. Now nothing was standing in its way from killing all of the puny humans disturbing its sleep. With one swish of its head it gazed all of us in the eyes. (Or eye for its sake).

When it stared at me, it stared into my soul. Last time it was brief but this time I could feel it even stronger. Flashes of death, destruction, blood, screaming, past experiences all mushed together in one big blur. Zane. He was towering over me grimacing. Maggie. Jay. Something was wrong. Some of the images never happened. What was I seeing?

I had to break out of the trance. There was no way I was going to let that thing beat me. Happy thoughts, I said. Fiona. Yes, Fiona was the happiest thing I could think of. Her warm smile glaring down at me. The sweet smell of her strawberry perfume. Her eyes. Her eyes were staring right at me. Staring, watching. Almost…realistic.

"Rick," she smiled. "There you are."

"Fiona?" I asked stupidly.

"Who else, dummy?" she nagged. "You called?"

"No?" I said. "I didn't know I could call for you."

"You can't," she said. "I just know when you need me."

Okay, now I knew I was defiantly *muy loco*. I hated that she was dead but that doesn't stop me from freaking out when the dead talk to you. And another thing, do you think Fiona and I are technically still dating even though she's a ghost? Sigh.

Guardian problems

"Well, I do need you," I said. "I always need you."

"AWWWWWWWWH!" I swear if Fiona's eyes could turn into hearts, they would.

"Haha," I said quickly. "I need to fight or get away from The Nightmare. I'm guessing you can use your ghost powers or whatever to help me."

"I can't," she sighed. "It doesn't work like that. But I can give you some advice."

"Advice?" I asked.

"Yeah," she said. "You can't kill it. You can seal it, though."

"Seal?" I said. "I need Master and -"

"You always doubt yourself," she sighed.

"I have to," I said. "Even though I go off instinct, I gotta reflect."

"You talk too much," she said.

95

"It's not my fault," I started. "I-"

"Rick, I'm fading," she said. "You can figure it out, I trust you." She pecked me on the cheek. Her image started disappearing. "I'll be back when you need me."

"Wait, don't go," I begged.

"Bye, Rick," she laughed.

She waved as she evaporated from my conscious.

When I opened my eyes, everyone was still in a trance. I couldn't make a seal but I knew what to do. What was it, we were twenty feet underground? Good thing I had energy stored in my sword and in my suit. There were no other Earth Guardians and even if there were they'd be in a trance too.

I created a rock shield on my hands and punched through the stone in the floor. Then, I planted my hands firmly in the dirt. I stared at The Nightmare as I gathered all of my strength into my arms. I honestly forgot about the thing so I had to come up with another plan. "Hm, what to do," I thought as the giant, dark monster rocketed for my face.

Fire spewed from my mouth as hot as the sun itself. The Nightmare howled in horror as I kept the fire going. Then, guess what, I lifted the room into the air. Well, what I did was grab all of the Earth under the room and pulled. So, I had to keep pulling for twenty feet while trying to hold back an apocalyptic monster.

I wasn't going to make it, I was using too much energy trying to hold back The Nightmare.

I don't know if it was Fiona or the great Guardian in the sky but I saw Jay twitch. I had to wake him up. I had to.

"Jay!" I yelled. "C'mon, man, wakeup."

He stirred a bit.

Wakeup. Wakeup. Wakeup.

"Hnhhh," Jay moaned.

"Jay!" I yelled, exerting all of my strength.

His eyes sprang open. He looked around a bit, confused. Then, he gasped a little when he saw the Nightmare. I didn't have time for him to ask questions. I needed action. Like a Hollywood movie.

"Jay," I had to briefly stop the fire. "Flamethrower your mom."

He sat there for a second. But Jay was trained. He knew what to do. But after that, he used all of his might to set The Nightmare on fire. That gave me more energy to lift us up to the heavens.

The roof broke off once we hit grass. Sunlight spewed into the room which blinded me. The Nightmare must have not liked the sun because it screamed even louder and burrowed down back into its ruins. I unplanted my hand from the ground and dusted them off. Yeah, that's right, I beat The Nightmare.

"Sure not going back in there," I said to Jay. "I don't even care if the Crystal is in there."

He threw up his deuces, "Tru."

The trembling from the ground moving so much aroused the rest of the Guardians. Elisa still did not rise and I was kind of concerned. Not really, honestly. I was sure she was okay.

"What?" Maggie looked around. "Where is the Nightmare?"

"I beat him," I said. "Something you couldn't do. Kind of in vein, though, because Big Mama didn't have the Crystal."

"No matter where it is, you won't get it," Maggie said as she picked up Elisa's body. "I have no more time to waste with you idiots. Let's go, Shadow."

"You're not even going to stop to fight us?" Jay taunted.

"The Shadow has no more business here," Seth grunted. "If you get in our way again we will eliminate you."

"Is that a promise, Roughneck?" I asked. "Or a threat?"

"Both," he said as The Shadow disappeared into the jungle. Their thick boots hit the leaves of the trees with loud noises.

"Hm," Antoine said as he dusted off his pants. "We don't have any other leads to the Crystal. Do we follow them?"

"Well," I sighed. "Let me put it this way." I had to gather my thoughts so my speech would come out right. "If we don't follow them we have to go back to Bikini Atoll with nothing. If we follow them then we could possibly find out where the stone is AND we can try to get rid of this little organization they have going on."

"Hm," Sam said. "Well I'm in for some more action. How about you guys?"

"I'm game," Brooke said immediately. "Antoine is too."

"Hey, you can't decide for me," Antoine protested. "But yeah, I'll go."

"And you know I like action," Jay smiled. "You don't even have to ask me."

"Alright then," I looked in the direction The Shadow had headed. They were headed back to the United States of America. I also thought that if we went back to the U.S. we might get spotted. But then again, it was time for me to put a stop to all of this hiding once and for all. "If we're going to follow them then we need to hurry up. They're getting away."

CHAPTER XI

Uncle Eddy's

Friday, August 10th, 2068. The smell of beignets, pronounced benyays, and hot chocolate told me I had returned home. I looked out of the window of Uncle Eddy's and remembered why I left. The streets were still filled with construction crews trying to fix ruined buildings from Zane's War. That just goes to show how quickly things can change.

Dane and the rest of them were scheduled to meet my little recon group in a few minutes so we decided to have brunch. Beignets can be eaten anytime so I wouldn't have really called it brunch, it was just a meal. Dane and them were in another press briefing to try to compensate for the last one. The humans cancelled the search warrant they had on us because they wanted a private, civil discussion.

Oh, and don't worry. We tracked down The Shadows exact location so we were all good. We needed a break (and showers) before we went to go fight the head hydra. Not only that, Sam was starting to miss her big fellah and I kinda did too. He was the only person in our original group who didn't go so it just didn't feel right fighting creatures and zombies without him.

Most of the customers had moved away from The Freak Table because, well, humans weren't too friendly with us Guardians at that time. Pssh, if I were them I wouldn't be either. Out of nowhere, Zane, a Guardian, goes and trashes the whole place and leaves them to clean up. And when the humans tried to talk to us, Maggie and her crew, Guardians, had to come in and ruin that too. First contact with Guardians since Medieval times and someone had to screw it up. Oh, and then they blame a fifteen year old and his posse.

The door of Uncle Eddy's squeaked opened as familiar faces entered the joint. Dane, with his stocky figure, walked in first. Behind him came Lance and Sabrina. They didn't have Tensar with them because I assume they didn't want to freak out the humans anymore than we had already. Their boots thumped on the ground as they pounded over to our table. Dane, with his big brown eyes, looked over in our direction and immediately put on a comical smile.

"Rickaaaay," Dane laughed as he spread his arms out.

"Dane the Mane," I said as I stood and greeted him.

"I missed you, brother," He said as he patted me on the back. "Glad you guys are all in one piece." I laughed and said barely as I greeted the rest of the Guardians. They all smelled fresh of seawater and sand. Sabrina had a sunburn on her arm that she got from

101

tanning too much. And you knowing me, I poked it a couple of times.

"Ey, don't tell me that's Dane I hear!" A voice asked from the kitchen of the shop.

"Yeah, Unc," Dane yelled back. "Who else would it be?"

A short, pudgy man wobbled from the back with a white chef's hat on. He bore glasses on his nose and his white apron was covered in powdered sugar that spread to all of his clothes. He had a cheery smile on his face that was not hidden by his spotty gray beard. I could tell that it would take a lot to bring down that man's spirit.

"Dane!" The man exclaimed. "Boy, look at you. Last time I saw you you were about as tall as a Nebbler." He then looked over at the rest of us. "Oh, and you're not gonna introduce me to your friends?"

"Riight, riiight," Dane said embarrassed. "These are my Guardian friends and guys, this is my uncle, Uncle Eddy."

"Oh, nice place you have here," Sam said. "I never knew who the man behind the name was."

"It's been me the whole time," Uncle Eddy said proudly. "Love it. Wouldn't want another job. C'mon in the back. We got some business to take care of, youngins. I don't want these humans meddlin' in Guardian business."

"We don't want them more than they already are," Lance remarked. "Disgusting."

Uncle Ed led us to the storage room in the back of the shop. It smelled of sugar and lemons. I don't know why, but magic smells like lemons and candy canes. Lemons and candy canes are life.

Antoine put a sound barrier around us for extra protection. Even though Uncle Eddy said we wouldn't be overheard we had to take extra precautions. Trust me, there was no room for mistakes. The last time I didn't use a sound barrier, I heard Jay singing in the shower. Trust me, you don't want to hear Jay singing in the shower.

"Alight, let's start," I said. "How did the conference go?"

"Terrible," Lance spat. "There was a reason it wasn't televised this time. The human government wants us to give over all of our intel on Zane and Maggie. Of course, we refused without hesitation. The humans didn't take a liking to that so they decided to bombard us with more questions. We gave them brief intel on some of the creatures they might encounter and treatments for some bites and stings that don't require Guardian medicine."

"What is the outcome of our status with them?" I pushed.

"Well, it is quite tricky," Lance said. "The humans see the Guardians as a whole and associate us with The Shadow. Right now, they are neither with nor against us. But they do have reason not to trust us considering that two out of the three encounters we have had with them were hostile."

"Those humans," Uncle Ed started. "You can't trust them anyhow."

"We told them we could take care of our own problems," Dane said. "They still insist that if we interfere with their society again, they will become hostile."

"That's not good," I said sadly. "Our mission wasn't a complete success either."

"Are the rumors that I've been hearing true?" Uncle Eddy questioned. "Is it true that someone is after The Crystal of Life?"

"Yeah," I said. "That's what our mission was about. How did you hear about it?"

"Retired Guardians hear everything," Uncle Ed laughed. "You youngins will soon learn that you can't keep secrets for very long from Guardians."

"Well," I said surprised. "Long story short, we went to a ruin, found The Shadow there and The Nightmare. We barely got out of there alive. And we still don't know where the Crystal is, but we know where The Shadow's hideout is."

"And now we're stuck," Dane said. "That's why I wanted to come see you, Uncle Ed."

"Eh, what does an old Guardian like me have to offer, Dane?" Uncle Eddy sighed.

"Knowledge," Dane said proudly. "And The Stash." I hoped that The Stash was a stash full of Meat Lovers' Pizza.

"Right!" Uncle Eddy had an epiphany. "I haven't used that thing in so long I almost forgot about it." Uncle Eddy began to wobble over towards the meat locker. Why in every story there's always a meat locker that's always holding some big secret? I know why, because meat makes Meat Lovers' Pizza. And Meat Lovers' Pizza is the key to everything.

"We don't sell meat," Uncle Ed said as he closed the meat lockers door. "But it's good for freezing dough and hiding stuff." He laughed.

"Where's this stash?" I asked.

"Right here,"

Uncle Ed lifted his arms and out of thin air, The Stash appeared. The Stash must have been covered by a veil made of air and water so I had suspicions that Uncle Ed was a dual Guardian. The Stash was weapons and gadgets. There were things there that I didn't even know what the function of them were. I was mostly interested in the instant popcorn maker next to the backscratcher.

"Can we borrow what we want?" Antoine asked.

"Take it all," Uncle Eddy said happily. "I don't need any of it anymore."

"Won't be necessary," I said. "This is going to be a stealth mission. I'm only taking three of you with me."

"Who said you got to be the boss?" Jay asked. "If I want to go, I'm going."

"That's your problem," Lance said. "You make rash decisions based off of emotions. You're not fit to make any decisions."

"Hold up," Jay said angrily. "Who asked for your input, midget? Go back to Georgia."

"Honestly, I'd like it if you went with him," I hissed.

"Alright, all of you, stop it," Dane yelled. "You're all being stupid."

"With all respect, I am the leader of my Squad," Lance attacked. "We don't have to be here right now."

"Leave," Jay said quickly.

"No," I said. "Stay. Jay's being a idiot."

"Why should we?" Sabrina asked. "You guys literally bump into death and shake its hand every day."

"Right," Lance said. "I forbid any of my Squad from going on this mission."

"What, no," I protested. "I need a Water Guardian with me. Brooke is coming."

"No," Lance said. "Brooke is going back to Bikini Atoll."

"I'm going with Rick," Brooke held her ground. "I do what I want."

"Fine, traitor," Lance said. "Antoine, what about you?"

"Um, um," Antoine hesitated.

"Antoine's been through a lot," I said, saving him. "I don't want him to be troubled anymore. He needs to rest."

"Good," Lance said. "When you guys can appreciate us, you know where we are. Brooke, I thought you were better than this. The rest of you, let's go," Lance ushered his posse to leave with him as he swaggered out of the meat locker.

What a jerk.

"Well," I started. "That escalated quickly. Sam, go with them. I think you deserve a rest too."

"Yeah, my butt still hurts," she said as she followed behind them. "Bye guys!"

"Bye," I said waving to her.

"So, it's just you four?" Uncle Eddy asked.

"Yeah, I guess so," Dane said. "Unc , any advice?"

"Yeah," He said. "Just remember what you're fighting for and you'll be fine. Not everyone is purely evil nor purely good. There's always a reason behind every ones actions."

"If you think about it," I said. "That is true."

"Wise words, Mr. Eddy," Jay said. "And thanks for the weapons."

"No problem," He chuckled. "And it's Uncle Eddy to you."

CHAPTER XII

Sister, Sister

You would have thought that an evil organization's hideout would be somewhere menacing. Usually, they're on mossy lakes or deep somewhere in a forest. I guess I got the hipster villains. These crazy fools had their secret lair right in the busiest part of Miami's business district. At least the beaches we nice there, though.

My rule was to not use any Guardian powers until we were inside of the building. That was the easy part. The hard part was getting in without drawing any attention. Saying that, they didn't make it quite easy for us. Ya know, with all the people walking around and staring at us.

Lucky for us, Uncle Eddy had installed sneak suits into our outfit. The only problem, though, was that they only work for five minutes at a time. And, and we would still cast shadows and make noise. But I wasn't complaining.

We were on that Mission Impossible type stuff. I mean, climbing buildings in invisible sneak suits was pretty cool. You don't just go up to anyone and they'll tell you that they actually did that. I kinda had to but it's still the principle of the thing. Shutup, I know I'm rambling.

"Don't. Look. Down," I warned as we climbed the windows of the massive building.

"That's the last thing on my mind," Jay said beside me as he burned a large hole into the glass. "Hurry in, it's almost been five minutes," he urged us. The level we snuck into was empty, lucky for us. Our sneak suits faded as Brooke landed softly onto the floor.

"Okay," I said in almost a whisper. "We're in here to find out where the Crystal is and then get out. Now, if that means getting someone hurt, so be it. But if we can avoid it, try not to be seen."

"Got it, chief," Dane said with a stern face. "Can I make the building collapse after we find out where the Crystal is?"

"Are you nuts? No," I said suppressing my anger. "Let's get into the air vents so we can have access to the entire building."

"I don't think I can fit in there, I've been eating a lot," Brooke said sadly.

"Yeah, right. You could be a fashion model with that body," I smirked.

"Awh," she said. Bingo.

Okay, so I was skinny and I could barely fit in the air vent. The rest of them were squished like sixty clowns in a clown car. Good thing I wasn't planning on using weapons in there because we would have been out of luck. But you know, that's just me being precautious.

What I always wondered was how could someone afford a building like that without a steady income? I mean, if you're out to destroy the world I know you wouldn't contribute to the work force of it. Maybe they get the money from inheritance or they brainwash someone to get their money. Didn't I, like, blow up Zane's joint last year? Maggie must have gotten this one off the insurance money.

I raised my hand to tell the others behind me to halt. We had come to a room and it was visible through the air vent. Seth and Lunk were walking around doing usual business. Seth was reading a map that looked like it was the downtown area of Miami. Lunk by the look on his face was obviously bothered by something; he nervously paced across the room. Seth noticed this and looked up from his map.

"Brother," Seth said in his rough voice. "We have not had much time to talk since I've returned. What's bothering you?"

Lunk sighed and gathered his thoughts. His pacing stopped abruptly as he leaned on a table. "Father would not have wanted Maggie to lead us," he began. "You are next in the bloodline. We should not be listening to this brat."

"Don't be one sided, brother," Seth said calmly. "Father did not know when that witch's spell would lift so he passed on everything to Margaret. Even though she is not the eldest, she has leadership within her."

"But if not you, it should have been me," Lunk protested. "Maggie doesn't even have *real* Guardian powers. At least I have some."

110

"Margaret has her sword," Seth replied. "Even though she was chosen to succeed father, she chose me to be second in command. This does not matter, anyway. Father will be returning as soon as we find The Crystal of Life and everything will be back to normal."

"Yeah, right," Lunk said sarcastically. "That boy Rick and his posse' of rats are around every corner we turn. He's the reason we're in this situation, anyway."

"He got lucky with father," Seth said. "I've only have had a chance to battle with him once but luck took his side again. Plus, I am still weak from the witch's spell."

"Tell me again how you got trapped by such a dumb creature," Lunk asked.

"Witches are quite smart, brother," Seth corrected. "This one in particular, very sly. As you remember, I traveled to Europe to acquire vampire blood for an experiment I was working on. Upon arrival, I heard rumors of a lone witch who was said to have all the blood I needed for a small fee. I took the opportunity and went into her lair unarmed. Turns out that the small fee was something I could not afford. The witch tricked me, though, and said she would bargain with me. She twisted her words and I agreed to become her test subject for the next five years for one bottle of vampire's blood."

There was a thump in another room. Seth looked at Lunk confused. "I thought I told you to destroy those extra Guardians. I knew my power was being drained more than it should."

"Sorry, I wasn't thinking," Lunk said as he walked to the door.

"And that's how ignorant Guardians die," Seth replied.

111

The two scurried out of the room, slamming the door behind them.

"Let's move," I said when I made sure it was clear. "Did the rest of you guys hear all of that?"

"Yeah," Dane said. "Sounds like those imitation Guardians are Earth Golems."

"Can you do that?" I asked.

"Nope," Dane said sadly. "Takes years of practice. And I don't have time to practice when I'm spending all of my free time climbing in vents."

I didn't care about the Golems. I knew why they wanted the Crystal of Life so badly. If they brought Zane back then he would be crazier than he was before. But that got me thinking. What if I could revive Fiona? I knew Headmaster and Master wouldn't allow it so if I did it I would have to keep it a secret but like Uncle Ed had said, you can't keep secrets from Guardians for that long.

I halted my group again as we approached another non-vacant room. My eyebrows raised as I realized the two figures in this room were Maggie and Elisa. I urged the Guardians closely because I knew some good intel was going to come out of this. Maggie looked pretty mad so I knew she was going to blurt out a couple of things.

"You said you were positive the Crystal was there," Maggie raged. "Instead, we found that thing that almost killed everyone."

"I know, sis," Elisa coughed. "My mistake." Elisa looked as if she was on the brink of death. She was laying down on a white couch with regular clothes on. Her hooded cloak was hung neatly on a coat rack by the door. Strangely, the cloak wasn't black anymore. It was pure white.

"Big mistake," Maggie corrected. "I don't know if your powers are ever coming back. What did you say happen again?"

"The Nightmare took them," Elisa said shamefully.

"What would that thing want with your powers?" Maggie asked. "Father said you were born with them."

"What does he know?" Elisa asked. "He's not our true father."

"He might as well be. He practically raised us from birth. We may not be Guardians by blood like Seth and Lunk but we were raised as ones." Maggie said.

"They shouldn't even be called Guardians," Elisa laughed. "I'm glad father drank that poison that hindered the powers of his children. That makes us evenly matched."

"I fear that the poison's effect has long faded," Maggie sighed. "I've been thinking. Before we head to Atlantis I want to give you something."

"What is it?" Elisa asked, intrigued.

Maggie then turned toward a long box that was resting on the table. As she opened it, the shine from the blade of the new sword brightened the entire room. Elisa stood as she realized what Maggie's gift was and smiled happily.

"You've been training a lot," Maggie said. "I think you deserve it."

Elisa then grasped the sword and waved it around. "Do you think it will hold off The Nightmare in Atlantis?"

"Why would it have to hold off The Nightmare in Atlantis?" Maggie questioned.

"Um, no reason," Elisa flinched. "I just have a feeling that it should."

"I have a feeling you're lying to me," Maggie gritted her teeth. "Is this connected with the loss of your powers?"

Elisa did not respond. Maggie went over her thoughts as slow as she could. I could see the questioning and realization on her face every time her brain came up with a new hypothesis. Elisa just sat back, nervous.

"Did you really thing the Crystal was in those ruins?" Maggie asked. "Even though I saw no connection, I took your word for it because, you know, you're my sister."

Elisa didn't respond again.

"Elisa, do you hear me?" Maggie waved her hand in front of her. "Hello?"

"You don't understand," Elisa said suddenly. "You never will unless you change."

"Change what?" Maggie demanded.

Elisa then looked Maggie directly in the eye. A tear dropped from Elisa's eye. Then she slapped Maggie in the face.

"Are you nuts?" Maggie yelled.

114

"It may not control me anymore but I can still hear echoes of its presence," Elisa said. "You don't understand. It gets what it wants. I had to do it, Maggie. It's been searching for so long. It was getting tired of waiting for so long."

"I don't understand," Maggie admitted. "Speak in English, Elisa."

"I told The Nightmare where the Crystal was!" Elisa blurted out. "I had to." She sobbed.

"You...what?" Maggie said in disbelief.

"If you were a Disturbed you would understand," Elisa backed away from her sister.

Maggie's eyes widened. A few light bulbs went off in her head. "I always thought you were born with those powers. I don't know how many times I've heard the story of The Nightmare. I just can't believe. My own sister. Why were your powers so advanced from the other Disturbed?"

"It said I was special," Elisa recalled. "It knew I needed them. It made me feel like it really cared about me. But that thing doesn't care about anyone. It will kill anything." Elisa tightened the grip on the sword she just recieved. "That's why I can't let you go to Atlantis. I tried to discourage you from going but I guess you won't back down."

"Elisa," Maggie cried slowly. "Don't make me have to kill you."

Elisa then skillfully swung her sword at Maggie. With lightning speed, Maggie blocked the attack with her sword, which was an inch from her face. Elisa had striked to kill. She was serious.

They both retreated and striked again. It was a battle of strength as they pushed their swords toward each other. Once they decided they were evenly matched, they let go.

Maggie swung at Elisa's knees, which made Elisa jump to avoid the blow. Landing on her feet, Elisa took the chance to strike again. Maggie was too slow to react and received a gash on her face as punishment.

"How?" Maggie asked as she swung again. "Elisa, stop."

"I can't. You're going to hurt yourself," was Elisa's response. The girls battled with strength. It was not clear whether there was a winner or a loser. They stumbled over tables and knocked down Elisa's cloak. When Elisa tripped over her own cloak, Maggie finally took the upper hand. Maggie took the opportunity to take the battle outside of the room where I thought she might have more of an advantage. I could still hear the clashing of their swords echo all in the hallway.

I hesitated and popped open the grate that led to the room below. I jumped down and landed softly on the floor. I heard the girls fighting right outside the door so I stayed quiet. My concern was not with their little family quarrel but with finding the Crystal.

When the sisters were far enough away, I quietly closed the door. I signaled for the rest of the group to come on down to the Crystal Is Right. They all stretched their bodies and thanked God for being out of that cramped space. I saw dents in the vent that Dane had left when he had to stretch earlier.

The room was trashed, no doubt. Lucky for us, though, the laptop with all the important files on it was not. Maggie and Elisa seemed happy, too. They were even yelling and junk all the way in the other room. I kept looking back to make sure they weren't going to burst into the room chopping people up.

I let Sam have at it with the computer. I told the rest of the crew to follow me outside to check up on Maggie and Elisa. They weren't hard to find considering that outside the door was an open area living room type deal. There was a couch in the pit in the middle of the room with a nice view of the busy Florida streets down below.

There was a wall beside the door so I urged my crew behind me to watch all the action unfold. The sister's heavy metal clashing against each other over and over ran chills up my spine. The girls hadn't stopped since they began. It wasn't my fight though, I was just there to watch.

"Elisa," Maggie said out of breath. "I'm begging you, stop. I don't want to kill you."

"I know you don't, you're weak on the inside. WEAK!" Elisa let the last word linger.

Maggie was shocked with silence but she continued to strike. With one good blow, Maggie knocked the blade clean out of Elisa's hand. Maggie swallowed hard as she realized what she had done. Before, there was only one tear in her eye. Now, she was crying.

Elisa got down on her knees with her arms spread. "Do it," she urged. "Do it if you aren't weak."

Maggie tried to hold back her tears. "Sis, I-"

"Excuses," Elisa interrupted. "You would have done it by now if you were going to do it." Maggie was silent. "But you know, I planned for your weakness," Elisa stood up, eyes pried on Maggie.

She then reached inside of her back pocket on her jeans. She brought out a little detonator that looked like a projector remote.

"What is she doing?" Brooke whispered.

"I don't know yet," I whispered back.

"Elisa, put that down," Maggie begged.

"No, I won't," Elisa protested. "If you come too close to me, I'll set it off." I tensed myself. "It doesn't matter, though. Whenever it touches that wall over there, the rest of the charges I set up around the building will go off. No, I don't want to kill you. But this will get rid of all of your technology. That way, you'll have no way to get to Atlantis."

"You wouldn't," Maggie said.

"I am," Elisa replied. "If I were you, I'd start running now. Seth and Lunk will be fine. They'll hear it before it comes to them. But this area...ka-boom."

"Elisa, don't," Maggie begged her again as Elisa bagged into the wall. Elisa was serious. We had to get out of there. There was no need for secrecy anymore. I had to get Sam out of that room. I urged the rest of the Guardians to go forward as I went to go get Sam.

"Sam!" I yelled. "Screw the notes; the whole place is going to blow!" Maggie and Elisa were shocked at our sudden appearance. Elisa was still bagging up into the wall.

"Rick! I'm so glad you're here," Elisa smiled. "I assume you've heard everything. I'll warn you like I warned my sister; don't go to Atlantis. Leave the Crystal alone."

"No," I said simply. Sam had joined us by now. We were all standing by the glass overview with Maggie. Elisa was so close to the wall. Rushing with adrenaline, Sam burst the windows open.

"Fine," Elisa said. She was only two steps away from the wall.

"Sis," Maggie cried as we all stepped onto the ledge of the window.

"Don't," Elisa hissed. "Just remember, Maggie," She was one step away. We all tensed ourselves. "No matter how much you love him, he won't love you back."

"NOOOOO!" Maggie yelled.

We jumped.

I heard the thump of the detonator hitting the wall.

I skydived on my back as I saw the building burst into explosions. Like Elisa had said, the bombs went off on the upper levels first, and then slowly made their way down the building. If it wasn't deadly, it would have been elegant. I had no time to stare at the building, though. I didn't know how far I was from the ground.

"Deploy Smart Parachutes," I said as I faced the approaching ground. As the rest of them deployed their parachutes, I waited a little bit longer. I spotted Maggie, unconscious, hurtling extremely fast to the ground. I felt sympathy for her; she was a kid just like me. Like the rest of us. I spread my arms out towards her. I caught her with wind hands and gently sent her floating towards a bridge far away from the explosions.

I pressed a button on my suit and I felt the heavy force of the parachute behind me. I ordered the squad to parachute far away from

119

Maggie and the building. Once we landed, I checked to make sure everyone was okay. No one was really hurt except Sam, she got cut by glass on her arm. Dane was happy to patch that up for her.

"Never thought at fifteen I'd be jumping out of exploding buildings," I tried to lighten the mood.

"Every day's a challenge with you, dude," Dane said.

"How exciting," I said sarcastically. "Sam, did you get anything?"

"Nothing we already didn't know," she replied.

"Well, now we know where the Crystal is for sure this time," I said.

"Atlantis? Really? We're not fish dude," Jay said. "And some of us don't really function properly in water."

"I can," Brooke said happily. "Sounds fun."

I looked at the horizon of the nice sunset. It reminded me of all the times Fiona and I spent dates watching the sun go down and watch the moon rise to take its place. That was the only reason I was going to Atlantis, to get to do that again. I sighed, hoping for the possibility.

"Next stop," I said proudly. "Atlantis."

CHAPTER XIII

Confessions

"No, absolutely not."

"Why, mommy?" I asked, begging her.

"I don't care if you're going to Atlantis or jumping out of buildings but riding a motorcycle is out of the picture," she said.

"I'm fifteen," I explained. "I should be able to drive by now and I'm not going to hurt myself. And it's not even a normal motorcycle. It's a Guardian one with all kinds of stuff on there to protect me."

"I don't care if it's a flying pig, Rick," my mom said.

"But Chris-"

"Chris will be fine," Mom said. "He's not the one who has to ride it."

"Fine," I said, giving up. "If we need a ride and don't have one, you're coming to pick us up."

"Okay," my mom said un-amused as she continued cooking.

Well, there goes my plan to burst into Atlantis with my sweet new motorcycle. According to Master I had to have BOTH of my parents' permission to ride. Of course, my dad said yeah. My mom, though, she's a tougher cookie to crack. I didn't see the harm in riding my motorcycle but mom knows best, I guess.

Finally, I got to spend a Friday afternoon not fighting Guardians or mystical creatures. What I planned to do was just chill in my room until it was time to go to Atlantis. As usual, though, I had to get some Guardian crap done. My two teams had to be de-briefed on everything since we left Bikini Atoll and we have to figure out how we were getting to Atlantis.

Master gave us an hour to go and rest our minds. My mind was still on active duty, though. I ran around the island for about ten minutes trying to tire myself out. After that didn't work, I practiced with my sword. I decided to name it Flaire because of the way it glittered when I waved it. I actually had fun with Flaire for a bit but then I realized the time and I went to go visit my parents.

As I looked around, I realized how friendly Bikini Atoll had become to me; the palm trees swaying in the wind, the subtle feel of radiation from decades ago, and the smell of fresh salt water. In some ways, Bikini Atoll was better than B.R.S.M.B.S. More freedom at the Atoll too. Not to mention our own cabins with free cable.

To say the least, I was happily enjoying my day. I was taking a stroll down a makeshift sidewalk along the edge of one of the atolls in the late morning. It seemed relaxing enough since yesterday, I witnessed a suicide. Well, look at me, I'm fifteen and I've seen so much that I really didn't care about death anymore. That's the life of a warrior, I guess. Some things of the warrior life I enjoy, though, like having advanced hearing.

"I just don't understand," Brooke said in a hushed tone. Her voice echoed through the area but she wasn't close enough to be talking to me.

Quickly, I hid myself behind some bushes as her voice approached my ears. As I spread the shrubbery with my hands, two pairs of legs came into view. Brooke's nice pale legs and Jay's muscular tan legs came to a stop and they were at my full attention.

"Why Rick?" Jay asked. "He farts in his sleep, you know?"

"Jay, I'm being serious," Brooke responded.

"I am too."

"You're not helping the situation," Brooke started. "Is there something wrong with me? Did I hurt him somehow?" By the end of that, she was beginning to cry.

"The only way you hurt him is by being here," Jay finally said.

"What?!" she sniffed.

"You never had that much time to get to know Fiona," Jay said calmly.

"Yeah," Brooke cried. "What about her?"

"I can tell that you remind him of her. Just a little." Hm, well, that's best friends in a nutshell for you. I didn't have to say anything and Jay knew about my dirty little secret. And no, I couldn't deny it. Ever since the first day I met Brooke, I noticed the resemblance that made Fiona slightly jealous. I still hadn't recovered from my loss and thinking of Brooke as Fiona #2 was my way out of what would have been a great depression.

"That's…okay. As long as he's happy." Brooke sobbed a bit more and slowly I heard her boots walk away from Jay, leaving Alonso alone. Never had I felt such sadness in my heart for Brooke. Right then and there I realized my wrongs. Still, somehow, those wrongs still felt right to me. I had to move on from Fiona and Brooke was my pathway out of the tunnel. Unless, yes maybe, unless I could maybe somehow make our trip to Atlantis worth more.

A few minutes after Jay cleared out, I staggered from under the bush. Now, what if I could make the trip to Atlantis bring me more than just a pat on the back? I could actually use the Crystal for what it was made for: to bring back people from the dead. Selfish, I know. The lust, however, was killing me. The thought of Fiona's skin up against mine once again sent shivers through my body.

Was I hopelessly romantic? Maybe, just a little. You would be too if you worked for something your entire life and BAM, it just crumbles right in front of your face. I tried my best to hold it in since that day but even the Great Richard Raines couldn't control his feelings all the time. I remember when I thought my dad was the toughest man in the world. Then one day, I walked in on him crying. Not just crocodile tears, big, enormous ones. That was when I realized that even the toughest of us have to just let it all out sometimes.

I moped around for a little bit more. The meeting of how we were getting to Atlantis was suppose to start at five. Right then it was 4:30 and counting. That meant I was late, Guardians are expected to arrive early for everything. I dashed along the atolls with a quarter of my speed, dodging the palm trees and other Guardians as I flew by.

I arrived at four fifty-nine, technically not late. Everyone was already present; Jay, Dane, Sam, Brooke, Lance, Sabrina, Antoine, Keith, Arlene, Master and Headmaster. I don't know if you're imagining a boardroom with a giant table in the middle but it was nothing like that. If I had to describe it, which I kinda have to, it was more like Master and Headmaster trying to listen to the young Guardians complaints about our next mission into the unknown.

"No, I know most of you are not trained in any way to breathe underwater, we have that under control. We know what to do," Master was explaining to Lance and Sam. The rest is pretty pointless to recall but the jest of it were the Guardians going, "Blah blah blah, we can't swim to an unknown land." And then the Masters going, "Blah blah blah, we know, we have a solution."

Of course, I walked over like a boss and asserted the situation. "What's the problem?" I asked to everyone. As soon as I saw twenty thousand mouths open at once I raised my hand, "Not all at once, please."

"I'll go then," Lance spoke up. "Even if we know the Crystal is in Atlantis, how are we suppose to get there?" There was agreement among the other Guardians with slight amusement from the Water Guardians.

"I don't know," I said shaking my hands. "I just got here," I said sarcastically. I walked slowly around the whole group looking

125

at each one of my friends in the eyes, "You guys need to chill out, you know? We have a big mission ahead of us and y'all are arguing with Master and Headmaster like you know everything. I pretty sure they have something planned out."

"Actually," Master said as he parted the Guardians like the Red Sea. "We were waiting on Richard to explain to you our plan."

"Why couldn't we go on without Rick?" Lance asked, irritated.

"The answer is simple enough. I do not wish to repeat the same story twice when I can say it only once. I suggest you all take a seat and let Ravenhawl and I speak." Master said, lightly sitting on the soft grass. It seemed weird to me seeing an old man sit Indian style on the grass. I wondered if I had to help him get back up when he was ready to stand. The rest of the Guardians took their seats on the Earth, opened their ears, and were prepped to listen.

"First off, what do any of you know about Atlantis?" Master asked. Of course, everyone had heard the stories of the Lost City of Atlantis. Supposedly, a long time ago before man had a accurate way of writing history, there was an island somewhere above Africa that was of high stature. For many centuries, it warred with many ancient cities such as Athens and Greece. However, during one battle, they lost at a horrible cost. According to the myth, the ancient city sank in a single day and night of misfortune, never to be seen again. That was all the younger Guardians knew. The only thing I knew was that it was underwater.

"Most of what you heard is true," Master said. But there is one detail that is slightly off to protect the Guardians."

126

"I knew there had to be more to this…oh, God," Sam muttered.

Master acknowledged Sam's comment and continued, "Let's start from the beginning, Guardians created Atlantis, that is a fact."

"How come we never heard of this in history?" I asked. I remembered that this wasn't the first time the history books left out important things from Guardian history. I didn't like being left out of the loop. In this situation, knowledge was literally power.

"Because it was a disgrace to the Guardians, a memory we do not wish to recall. No more interruptions, please, we have little time as it is," Master said.

"Fine," I shut my mouth.

Master recited his story, "Atlantis was the first and only city made to serve as the capitol of the Guardians. This is where everyone would meet to discuss political matters and disputes. The ancient Guardians had a leader, Vetro, who was known to be very corrupt at times. Vetro favored the fire Guardians the most because of how simple fire was to him. His assistant, Saldare, was a young fire Guardian whom he kept around to assert his force since Vetro had no powers of his own. Vetro's lack of power made him a shoe-in for leader because it was thought that he would not side with one element.

"Years passed and the Guardians lived in peace, protecting the world from creatures and such, thinking nothing of Vetro. Vetro secretly created his plans while the Guardians were distracted with other matters. The only thing that can completely hinder fire is water, so for the fire Guardians to be in complete control, the leader had to eliminate the water Guardians.

"Vetro had banded together a group of non water Guardians who wanted to eliminate the Water Guardians also. Saladare was left out of the plan because he was not to be trusted and was too young to fight if he had to. So, Vetro set out to commence his plan. With his band of Guardians, they went to Atlantis's only beach which was located near the Water Palace.

"His plan was to get rid of the Water Guardians by raising the sea against its will and destroying the Water Palace which was built to enhance the water Guardians powers. All elements have a Palace to enhance their powers, which we still use today, even though we do not acknowledge them, and they are long forgotten. But yes, the Palaces are still active in Atlantis all of these years.

Vetro and his group raised the sea as they intended. What they did not intend was for the Water Guardians to notice and attack. A battle raged on as Vetro's Guardians still struggled for the sea to attack the Water Palace. The Water Guardians used a counter-measure to disrupt the attack on the sea and made it instead attack the beach. Saladare watched in horror as his leader tried to take out one of the elements. He couldn't stand the sight of such a thing and he joined the fight against his leader.

"When Saladare confronted Vetro on the beach, the sea became even more unstable. By this time, the other Guardians had heard all of the commotion and joined in. Saladare was outraged at Vetro and began attacking him with fiery fire. As the fire hit Vetro's flesh, so did the sea and all the sand that was being carried by the sea. Unstable, the sea began to engulf Atlantis rapidly, making it sink. The Guardians sensing the threat tried to protect Atlantis by pushing the sea back away from the land. While this did not work, it revealed that Vetro had been turned into glass on the beach.

"Saladare reacted fast and took the glass Vetro to the Lightning Palace. Saladare climbed the Lighting Palace and molted Vetro to the tip of the roof. He then called upon all of the Guardians to open the Lightning Palace's power and merge it with their own. Once that was completed, Saladare sacrificed himself and let the lightning element channel through his body and through the glass Vetro to create a barrier around Atlantis.

"As Atlantis sank, the Guardians fled their capitol city with no time to gather possessions. Wind Guardians carried those who could not fly or swim as they watched their city sink, still protected.

Of course, this is a disgrace to the Guardians who witnessed it. They swore to only reveal the story to a select few in case Atlantis was needed again. Like now."

"Wow," I said. "Guardians are pretty good at keeping secrets."

"Well, we were once a big secret to the humans," Dane pointed out. "That was a nice back story, Pops, but that doesn't explain how we're suppose to get to a city in the bottom of the ocean."

Master laughed, "It lies within the barrier."

"The whole city lies within the barrier. Could you be more specific, please?" I asked.

"There are already established portal connections in Atlantis, four to be exact, and we shall use one of them." Master said.

"Oh, so that was the plan all along," I said, excited. "When can we go?"

129

"We should have the portal ready tonight, you all should go get prepped for the journey." Master then stood. Even though he was old, he still had the strength of a Guardian. The muscles behind his dark, wrinkled shin was barely noticeable if he didn't exert force to them. He was probably stronger than the rest of us combined.

We all followed suit and stood as well. "Well, I don't know about you guys, but I'm ready. Let's get this over with," I said cheerfully.

"I'm with you," Lance agreed.

That was the first time Lance had sided with me in a while and I was shocked. Maybe Lance had gotten over not being in command now. Whatever the case, it slightly lifted some pressure off me. I had to worry about too many people and their feelings as it were, anyway. I didn't know myself how I was juggling all of that responsibility at once. Well, someone had to do it.

Slowly, everyone left the grassy field except Lance and Dane who had gotten into a dispute on who was hotter, Miku White or her sister, Kay White. They were having a concert later that afternoon with Bobby Richardson and few other famous Guardians. I laughed to myself as I thought that neither of them wouldn't even get a chance to date either of the sisters. To me, the day was till young and it gave me a chance to train more. Flaire and I would have a wonderful time slashing up wood and bricks for practice as I charged it with each element. My legs were aching to run for miles so I burst into a light jog along a path. I stopped soon enough though because something beautiful was blocking my way.

"Brooke," I said stopping in front of her. Her eyes were wide with some type of emotion that I couldn't decipher. She stood as if she had just been defeated in a long, arduous battle with someone.

Her hands were fidgeting at her sides and her hips rocked slightly in a circle. "What's wrong?" I asked.

"Rick..." she trailed off. She then embraced me in a tight hug. I squeezed her back and felt the brush of her hair on my skin. Her cheek was on my neck and I increased the pressure. We stood there in silence for a bit and I decided to close my eyes.

"What's wrong, Brooke?" I asked again, fearful of the answer.

Brooke broke the hug and stood close to me. Her crystal eyes gazed into mine with that same emotion she had earlier. Then, as her full lips parted, I realized what that emotion was.

Her voice was shaky as she spoke, "I think I love you."

CHAPTER XIV

Star Struck

Have you ever had one of those moments where the entire world just seemed to freeze entirely? You knew that the next action you made was going to affect your entire life. No, not just your life, another life entirely, too. I felt like that then. Brooke's eyes urged a response but my lips were dry with no answer.

Her voice did not tremble as she spoke, "I know you might not feel the same and I don't blame you." Still, I couldn't force my mouth to form words to talk back. "I just wanted you to know," she continued. Frozen, I stared into her eyes as she approached me curiously.

My arms grew a brain and I grabbed her by the waist. Then, as her ear approached my mouth, I whispered to her, "Brooke, you're perfect." Something stirred inside of me and I knew I actually wanted to say that to Fiona. My heart wanted to say Fiona.

My brain couldn't distinguish the difference between Brooke and Fiona.

"Don't say that," she said.

Her body shifted in my arms. "Why wouldn't I say things that are true?" Her mouth opened in response but I cut off her speech with a kiss. I had kissed Brooke before but this time was different. There was an extra ingredient added into the mix that gave it a bigger kick. This time it actually felt right.

After I let go of her she revealed a joyous smile on her face that only an angel could have. Her eyes glowed as brown as my skin in the pale sunlight which overcastted the trees that surrounded us. Slowly, as I looked at Brooke more, the cast of Fiona that I placed on her began to peel away, revealing the beautiful Brooke. At that moment, Fiona was gone from my mind and was replaced by Brooke. A sad, yet tragic, love story.

"Yo, Rick!" Jay yelled from behind Brooke. Alonso approached us with an air of swagger that only someone as arrogant as him could carry. Brooke and I broke our gaze and turned toward Jay as he stepped between us. "You coming to that concert later?" He asked.

"Um, maybe," I raised my eyebrows. I hadn't intended on going.

Jay then grabbed me by the wrist, ignoring Brooke. "Good, we need some bro time." He then shuffled me further away from my precious. I reached out my arm and told her that I'd be back and she smiled and waved in response. Then, before Jay and I turned the corner, she turned her back from us and walked in the opposite direction. Sigh, I hated to see her go, but I loved to watch her leave.

"What was that for?" I asked when Jay let go of me.

Jay dug his pointer finger into my chest. "I was saving you from yourself, idiot."

"I don't know what you're talking about," I responded.

Jay sighed and lightly tapped his foot on the grass. "You were about to tell her that you loved her. I know you don't, dude. I wasn't about to let you do that to yourself."

"You were eavesdropping, weren't you?" I said, shocked. "Some friend you are. Why don't you just stay out of my business?"

"If I did you'd be killed by Zane already," Jay said bluntly. "If he hadn't killed you by now, Fiona would have driven you crazy. Now I'm trying to save you before you go too crazy over Brooke, bro."

"I-"

"No, just listen to me for a second, okay?" Jay spat. "I've known you for forever. Your weakness is not fighting, explosions, or any of that crap. It's women, dude. You go all googly eyed for one chick and then when you get rejected you fall into a pit full of darkness. I've seen that look you get. Fiona wasn't the first and Brooke won't be the last. Promise me you won't do this again, will you?"

Jay's proposal made sense. But sometimes sense just doesn't make sense at all. I had Brooke in the palm of my hands and now my best friend was telling me to let her go. No, I couldn't do that. I had finally gotten over Fiona and now I wasn't about to let Brooke go. "I can't promise you anything, bro," I responded.

"You can't, huh?" Jay shook his head. "Go to the concert with me, I wanna show you something."

"Okay," I said. Then Jay and I made our way to our cabin.

Night concerts on the beach are the best. The flashing lights, the music, even the people made me feel alive. Jay and Dane had made sure to get us some good spots to enjoy the music and talk to the girls that were there. Of course, I wasn't worried about girls, I had Brooke. The boys still insisted that I went out and met someone new to get my mind off of her. I only agreed because they said they'd take me to go get Meat Lovers' Pizza before we left for Atlantis.

Bobby Richardson appeared on the stage in a flashy white suit. His overly white teeth stood out from his brown skin and made him look like a living, breathing, caricature. He looked the same since the last time I saw him. I bet he wouldn't even recognize me if I wasn't the Elemental Guardian. He raised his hand to the crowd and received a roar of applause. The band behind him ceased playing their song.

"Hey, everyone," Bobby said in his golden voice. "For those of you who don't know me, heh, my name is Bobby Richardson. I have been to this school plenty of times in the past but this time you guys are looking kind of *sandyyy*. (The crowd laughed at this.) Well, I'm just here to lighten up the mood. No battles this time, though. Last time they knocked the lights out! (More laughter.) But you guys sit tight and enjoy the show. Next up we got Miku and Kay White with their band, XXO! Give it up, everybody!"

The White sisters were two, very attractive Japanese teenagers. Miku, the older one, was slim with a smooth face and short Asian hair that went into curls. Kay was shorter and had more

135

weight to her but not the bad kind. Her hair went down in a black waterfall that covered the top of her eyes, which made her look like an anime character. Both sisters had a natural tan that made them look more Islander than Japanese.

"You checkin' the White sister out, bro?" Jay laughed. "They're way out of your league."

Dane hit Jay on the shoulder. "We're not here to discourage, remember? Rick, go for whichever you want. If I were you, though, I'd go for Miku." Miku then did a little trick with her guitar, which made it spray water everywhere. "She's even a Water Guardian, that's your type, right?"

"Yeah," I agreed. "I have a bad feeling about this, though."

"The last time you had a bad feeling it was only gas," Jay joked. "Shh, they're about to play."

XXO got the crowd pumped by raising their hands and screaming encouraging things. I had heard a couple of their songs before but I never knew they were around my age. Miku was the lead guitarist and the main singer while her sister was the second guitarist and the backup singer. Miku walked downstage toward the crowd and she got dozens of catcalls from the male audience.

"Alright, helloooooo Baton Rouge's School For the Mind, Body, and Soul!" Miku exclaimed with her attractive voice. The crowd went wild with more catcalls and whistles. "My name is Miku and this is my sister, Kay. We have a band called XXO and we're here to rock the night!" She then stepped back and joined ranks with her band. "Enjoy!" she gave everyone a little wink and then began playing.

"Wow, she's even more attractive in person," Jay drooled. "Rick, if you don't want her, I'll surely take her off your hands."

Lust, baby, lust. "I don't think one night will hurt," I smiled. "You can have Kay because your name rhymes with hers."

"And Dane will go home to his loving wife," Jay laughed. "It's a deal, bro."

"Whatever," Dane said. "Sam is probably drooling over Bobby right now. But yeah, when you guys make your moves, I'll be the wingman."

"It's funny because you can't fly," I joked. XXO finished their song and they thanked everyone for listening. They then began to start another song, this time with Kay as the lead singer.

"Kay sure can," Jay pointed as Kay did a trick in the air as the crowd went wild. "Alright, I'm fine with that."

"Hm, now the thing is…how do we get the attention of two very attractive super-stars?" Dane questioned.

"Dude," I gave him a smirk. "I'm the *Elemental Guardian*. I got this." We enjoyed the rest of XXO's song and then I began to formulate my plan. They began to play another upbeat one with Miku back in the lead.

Okay, I had a lightning charged dagger strapped to my belt. I had a safe bet that no one else in the crowd had one of those. I grabbed it from my side and flung it on stage, making sure not to hit anyone. The dagger hit the wooden stage with a clunk as the electricity flung from it, trying to escape the metal.

"Woah, dude," Miku exclaimed. "That was crazy. Who threw that?"

"My bad," I said acting embarrassed. I parted the crowd and made my way to the stage. I grabbed the edge and jumped up and landed in front of Miku. She looked hotter the closer you got to her. I saw no flaw on her face or body which kind of made me uneasy. "Did I ruin anything?"

"No, no. We were just wrapping things up," Miku's glint in her eyes changed as she looked again and realized who I was. "Wait, don't tell me! You can't be! The famous Rick Raines?"

"Only on days that end with "Y"," I laughed.

"I would have thought someone as important as you would be off doing some crazy mission or something." She turned back to the crowd. "Wow, guys, just wow. Everyone give it up for Rick!" The crowd clapped as I became embarrassed with recognition. I had never really wanted to be acknowledged for what I did last year because they brought back memories of...uh-oh.

"I believe we rocked you guys enough tonight. Thank you for having us, B.R.S.M.B.S! We'll see you guys next year, hopefully in an actual school!" She then blew the crowd a little kiss. XXO slowly departed the stage and left the stage all to me. Great, just what I wanted.

"Uh, hi," I said awkwardly. "I hope you guys enjoy this place. I sure do." I swear I could hear the crickets chirping in the background. "Well, it's about time for me to hit the old dusty trail..." I waved everyone goodbye and awkwardly picked up my dagger and left the stage, almost tripping on a step.

At the end of the stage, Dane and Jay were waiting on me, smiling. I laughed and high-fived Jay. "That couldn't have gone any smoother," I said. "Maybe if I had some beeswax but that's just maybe."

"Now we just gotta find out where those two went," Dane said looking around.

"I know where I'd go if I were a hot chick," Jay said.

"To look at yourself in the mirror?" I laughed.

"No, to the fountain," Jay pointed out. And there they were, the White sisters. Miku was sting on the marble fountain with her legs crossed showing off her stylish boots that went all the way up to her knees. Kay was a few feet away munching away on something that looked like a cookie.

Jay and I shoved each other to rush towards the sisters. Dane followed suit but at a slower rate. When we were in close enough range we stopped running and slowed to a brisk walk. I hurried over to Miku as Jay approached Kay. Once I saw that Jay had reached his target, I zoned him out of my eyesight and went for Miku.

"Hi," I said confidently as I sat next to Miku on the fountain. "I believe we met earlier."

Miku laughed as she looked over at her sister who was occupied with Jay. "What do you want?" she giggled.

"Maybe I want you," I said. "Or maybe I want nothing."

"You didn't come all the way over here for nothing," she said. "And you sure didn't throw that dagger up there on mistake."

"Oh, no, you found out my plan," I said sarcastically. "What shall I do now?"

"I don't know. What do you want?"

"Honestly, some pizza," I laughed.

"You're trying to impress me, aren't you?" she asked. "Well, it's not working."

"Do I have to try harder?" I asked.

"A lot," she laughed. "I am rock star material if you haven't noticed. It's gonna take more than another famous face to get to me."

"Hm," I paused. "I always wanted to kiss a rock star." I don't know what I was thinking. Maybe I wasn't thinking at all. All I know is that I leaned in to kiss Miku. No, I didn't get rejected. Miku leaned in, too, wanting to kiss me. But we didn't kiss, instead I was startled by a voice. A voice that called out my name.

"Rick!" Brooke yelled from a few yards away. Her expression was priceless "I cannot believe you!" Then she ran off.

"No, no!" I yelled as I got up and chased after her. I don't know what Jay, Dane or Miku yelled because everything became all blurry. I chased Brooke through the forest that was on the side of the beach. Even though I was fast, she had a head start ahead of me.

"Brooke! Brooke!" I yelled as I chased after her. I was catching up with her but not as fast as I wanted to. She tripped a few times over the tree roots and it gave me a chance to speed up. I had to duck under low branches because of my height which slowed me down a bit. I thanked God when we cleared out of the forest.

There, in the park, was Master and Headmaster tending to a swirling, white vortex that seemed omniscient to the area surrounding it. Master and Headmaster were looking the opposite direction when Brooke and I approached the portal.

"Brooke," I yelled. "I'm sorry!"

"No!" she continued running. "You aren't. don't say you aren't when you know you aren't!" She was looking back at me, which was a mistake. She tripped on a stray rock and fell. And what made this fall worse than any other fall, was that she fell straight into the portal.

I didn't think. I never think. I just acted. I felt the pressure on my feet as I sprang into a jump into the portal. Master and Headmaster had turned around by then and stood in shock. One of them yelled for me to not go into the portal but it was too late, I couldn't stop myself. The icy cold portal contacted my skin and I could no longer feel the breeze of Bikini Atoll. I felt nothing for what felt like eternity. Then, suddenly, I felt air again, an atmosphere. I was tumbling through the air…I couldn't seem to open my eyes.

Well, welcome to Atlantis.

CHAPTER XV

The Cry of the Sea

Hm, where were we?

Oh, yeah, I was FALLING THROUGH THE FREAKIN'
SKY. C'mon, Rick, you can think of something. Wait a minute, I'm
a superhero. I can swim, teleport, spit fire from my hands, and more
importantly, fly. And why were my eyes closed? God, Rick, I
needed to pull myself together.

I opened up my eyes and stared up at the…sky? What I saw
was not the sky I was used to. From where I was there was air.
Above that, there were no clouds, just darkness. The darkness was
trapped in some kind of transparent shield that surrounded my entire
vision. It stood as if that shield broke the darkness would engulf me
without hesitation. I shuddered at the thought and that gave me more
of a reason to face the ground.

Slowly, I turned my body like a rocket towards the ground. Then I realized, I was actually becoming Superman but cooler, of course. I wish I had a cape and some cool tights but black clothes and power gloves had to do. I was about twenty stories in the air going about a few hundred miles. If it wasn't a life or death situation it would have kinda been relaxing.

Something in the air pierced my ear. The breeze carried the sound swiftly past me and I barely realized that it was a scream. I increased my hearing and sight to the point where they were taking up most of my strength. If I hadn't though, I wouldn't have noticed the little dot below me spiraling out of control.

"Hang on!" I yelled to the falling Brooke down below. Now I really had to be Superman to save her. I stretched out my arms to make me fall faster and I stopped flying and just let physics do its job. I mentally high fived myself when I realized my plan was working. Any second and I should catch up with her and save her sorry butt. Her screaming didn't help my concentration at all and it made me feel like Spider-Man saving Mary Jane in those old Spider-Man movies.

"I got you," I said as I strapped my hands around Brooke. Now came the tricky part. We were only about ten story from the ground now and if I made one false move we were gonna splat onto the surface below. Brooke continued screaming in my ear and I had to ignore it to concentrate. No wonder superheroes always go mental; they have to deal with all of this crap.

The ground was visible now and I had to think fast. Remember when I said a long time ago that I really didn't need school? Well, that's because I'm a fast thinker. Not just with math and science and all that other school crap, I was street smart, too. I think from now on I'll call it superhero smart since they always seem to know what to do.

I created Earth Skin on my arm that was facing toward the ground and braced Brooke tighter. Hang on was the only thing I could yell to her before I shut my eyes as the ground decided to give my body a little kiss. Let me rephrase that, the ground gave me a rocky road… shut up, I know I'm lame.

The dirt gave way under the Earth Skin as we touched ground. From the landing point we slid a few feet and we slowed to a gruesome stop. I opened my eyes and was relieved to see that we were in fact on the ground and not dead. I looked at Brooke and saw that she was unharmed yet she had her eyes closed. I released my grip on her and rolled over a bit.

"It's over, you're safe," I said as I huffed in some air.

"Don't think that this changes anything," Brooke breathed. "I still hate you."

"I didn't expect anything less." I really didn't, you know girls. "Look. Let me explain myself."

"No, there's no need to explain. Your actions explain enough." I heard her turn her body away from me. Why do I have to be so stupid sometimes? I probably ruined whatever I had between Brooke in a few hours. I don't think any other guy is that stupid. But then again, I did just save her life.

"Can this wait until we get back home?" I asked. I turned to my side facing her. "We're kinda lost, here." I swear I saw steam come up from her nose. "No answer, hunh? Okay, I guess I'll just do this myself." I heaved myself up off the ground and my right arm throbbed with pain. I cupped the useless limb with my left arm and surveyed the area.

To the north, there was a forest. Luscious, green plant life encased the entire view with a sense of a thousand creatures. You could hear the chatter of the creatures roaming the forgotten forest with an air of business to it. From the top of the trees extruded the barrier that held back the swiveling darkness. The darkness shadowed the entire forest like an overhang in the night ready to protect the forest against any danger.

To the east, there was a beach. The shoreline was charred and destroyed with debris that stained the entire beach. White stones extruded from the sand that sparkled in the night. Again, as I looked up, the barrier held up the swaying darkness against the horizon of the roaring sea. The comparison of the sea and the darkness made it to where the two almost blended with each other. No, the darkness swayed back and forth just as the sea did. Then I realized that we were underwater. The darkness was actually water and the barrier was the one that Saladare created those many years ago.

"We're at the Southwest Gate," Brooke spoke up as she stood next to me. I guess she felt like getting up. "Master and Ravenhawl prepared me for this much."

"How do you know that?" I asked, curious.

She pointed towards the forest. "The Northwest Gate is surrounded with the Earth Forest to the south and the Wind Palace to the east. The Northeast Gate is north of the Fire Palace and east of the Wind Palace. The Southeast Gate is south of the Fire Palace and east of the Waters of the Guardians. And here we are, the Southwest Gate, surrounded to the north by the Earth Forest and to the east by the Waters of the Guardians."

"I figured there was only going to be one portal. Why didn't they tell anyone else about the rest?" I asked.

"Because they were going to go over all of this when all of us were together. I stayed with them as they created the portal and asked a lot of questions. When they finished I came to get you guys and then I saw…"

"Oh, Brooke." I went up behind her and grabbed her on the shoulder. "Can you please forgive me? It was a mistake. Jay made me do it."

"Get your hands off of me," she said. She shoved my hands off of her shoulders and stalked a few feet away. "Don't blame anyone else but yourself. I pour my heart out to you and you go and smooch with that rock band trash."

Then, like she hadn't eaten food in days and found some in her hands, she shoved her face in her hands and began crying. To the east, the roar of the sea grew louder with Brooke's sobs. If her emotions were powerful enough to sway an entire sea, I had messed up big time.

I walked a few steps closer to her. "Look, Brooke-"

BOOM. Thunder and lightning erupted from the sea behind us. "Get away from me!" Her face full of tears appeared gruesome in the artificial night. Even with her beauty, the sight scared me. I stepped back again and recollected my thoughts. The Crystal was there but I had no idea where to start looking. Brooke was having a mental breakdown and she was no help. Surely, I had some other options I hadn't explored. Oh, wait, I had about ten of them.

"We should wait here or the others," I said to Brooke. "It would be nice if you didn't make it rain."

146

She wiped away some of the tears from her face and sniffled. "Not likely."

"Why not?" I asked.

"When we fell through, the portal was unstable. They have to have to have a constant flow of energy to choose which portal to go through. They have no idea which one we went through. The odds are against us, they might come through any of the other three."

"They didn't tell you which portal we were supposed to go through?" I asked.

"They hadn't decided which one was best." Brooke then looked to the east. "I don't know if we would be going the right way, but I would love a walk on the beach right now."

"Fine," I agreed. "Let's go."

Until that night, I had never walked on a beach after dark. Actually, I hadn't walked on a beach until we went to Bikini Atoll. There was something mysterious about the tons of water above our heads and to the right of us. The light source seemed to be the barrier itself and it mixed in with the unforgiving darkness of the Atlantic Ocean. It sort of reminded me of how the sky is in Antarctica and the north pole. But this sky only had beautiful mixtures of black and a deep purple that moved with the sea.

"You know, the only thing beautiful than this beach is you," I said to Brooke as I gazed up at the sky.

"Nothing's going to work, Rick," she said. "I'm done with you." That shut me up. I had completely ruined my chances with Brooke. Jay got what he wanted, sort of. But you guys should know me by now. My motto should be pretty clear: "Never give up, never

147

surrender!" I actually think I heard that from somewhere but oh, well, I'm stealing it.

We had reached those shiny white stones I had seen earlier. They were buried deep into the sand ant it looked like it would take the strength of ten King Arthurs to pull them out. Curious, I stopped walking and decided to kick the sand off one of them with my feet. I bent down and pulled the rest of the stone out of the sand and Brooke screamed.

I think you call those femur bones or something? Whatever it was, it was sparkling white and picked clean of any flesh. It couldn't have been an animal bone because it was too big. Then I recalled Master's tale about the battle on the beach. He didn't mention anyone trying to pick up bodies while the whole place was drowning. My reaction was different than Brooke's though. Instead of screaming about the thing, I threw it far off into the distance.

"Ouch!" someone yelled from far away. My mind grew wild with confusion. Had Brooke and I been talking that long at the Gate that the rest of the gang had already caught up with us. Hm, well time does fly when you're arguing, doesn't it?

"It must be the rest of them," I said to Brooke. She nodded and we ran towards the voice.

"Hey, it's us, Rick and Brooke!" I yelled towards my friends. My boots left deep marks in the sand where I ran, eager to see people other than Brooke. She wasn't as enthusiastic as I was but she treaded along on the long run. She still had the look of anger on her face as she ran but it was beautiful anger. If only I could have captured that moment in slow motion and keep it on replay in my head.

148

We climbed a hill that was in the way and slowly made our way to the top. The view was gorgeous. And there, down at the bottom, was something not so gorgeous. Instead of Sam, Arlene or Sabrina speaking like I expected, it was the last person on Earth that I wanted to see.

Maggie.

"Oh, Rick, I'm glad you're here," Maggie laughed. "Not!"

I cursed to myself. "You'll follow me to the ends of the Earth if you can, won't you?" Maggie had brought along a few of The Shadow minus Elisa and some other lackeys. Lunk looked like a big hulk of struggle and regret while his brother, Seth, looked like he needed a hot bath. Still, though, six versus two was kinda unfair.

"You talk big for someone who it at a disadvantage, young warrior," Seth spoke. "We do not wish to fight you but we will if we must."

"By that I'm guessing you mean you want me to go home and let you guys get the Crystal," I said.

"Correct," Seth responded.

"Then," I slid out my sword. "No deal, bro." A trait of being a teenager is that sometimes you just don't give a crap. No negotiation, no compromise, just swords and fighting. I stayed true to my young mind and jumped off the sandy hill towards my enemies. Then my teenage brain had an epiphany; that was a bad idea.

I don't know who I was aiming for but in the end it didn't really matter. The Shadow dispersed and surrounded me when I landed. I swung my sword in a loose circle as to say "Get back!" to all of them. I caught one of the lackeys on the side and I ran towards him. With months a practice, I slid the lightning charged dagger from my side and tried to stick it into the already bleeding hole of the lackey.

Just a quick note, teenagers also seem to be very forgetful at times. Remember when I threw that dagger onstage at Miku and all of the electricity went out of it? Well, I kinda forgot to charge it back up. And kids, what happens when you try to send fire through a medal dagger? Well, it kind of melts.

I collapsed into the lackey and tumbled onto the sand. The metal was seeping into my power glove and I felt the hot metal scorch my hand. There was only one way I could get the metal off my hand. Good thing the lackey wasn't human. I engulfed the lackey's face with my power glove and heard his muffled scream. I could be a little more graphic but I wanna keep this story PG.

"There are many more where that one came from. They can be spared," Seth laughed. "Your campaign to fight us is very amusing." I don't know how or when this big guy walked or ran over to me but now he was only a foot away from me. His heavy feet made the sand scream under him as he approached me. Bending down, he grabbed me by the neck. Oh, great, my hand was still scorched and I had the other one trying to pry Seth's hand off my neck.

"You, Rick's comrade," Seth said to Brooke. "Go back and tell your friends the tale of how Richard Rains fell to my hands as you helplessly watched." Yeah, I would have heard Brooke's screams but the pressure in my ears suddenly increased tenfold. The force was so incredible that I even used my scorched hand to try to pry Seth off me. It was no use though. I was done for. Stars were forming in Seth's eyes as he chocked me out. They weren't shooting stars but I made a wish anyway.

Then a miracle happened.

Shooting stars, no, fireballs engulfed Seth's body and the pressure decreased from around my neck. He still held on as much as he could as he tried to pat the fire out with his free hand. I took this opportunity to get some cheep blows in his chest with my feet. Again and again, I banged his chest with my boots and finally he released me to try to save himself from the fire. When I landed on the beach, I realized that Brooke couldn't use fire. Someone else had saved me. Then, I heard my savior's voice.

"Don't touch my bro," It said.

CHAPTER XVI

Game Plan

"You!" Maggie screeched. The hatred in her eyes grew as she drew her sword. "I should have figured the rest of the Rat Crew was here."

"You crashed our party last time. We had to return the favor." Jay winked. "It's only common courtesy, cutie."

Maggie chose not to speak, instead, she charged. I knew Jay could handle himself so I focused back to my own life force. Seth was still tending to his wounds so that gave me time to get up off the ground and put up an actual fight. I wasn't gonna let Seth best me twice…and this time with a scorched hand. At least we were even now.

I drew back my hand and prepared to strike Seth with a Fire Hand but his own, gigantic arm stopped me. "No, Guardian, I do not wish to fight," he said. "This is pointless."

"What makes you think I will believe you?" I questioned, still ready to fight.

"Margaret is very impatient and hard headed." He looked up at me. "And so are you." Hm, he might have been right. I almost did just try to commit suicide. But if we let them go, they might have gotten to the Crystal before us.

"No," I said.

Then I attacked.

As big as he was, he wasn't suppose to move as fast as he did. My strike hit the sand and quickly extinguished. I felt his colossal hand on my back as he gave himself a platform to lift his body off of. Once he was a good bit above me, he shoved his hand into my back, sending me to the ground. Let me tell you, sand does not taste good.

"Ouch," I muffled. "I'm probably gonna have back problems when I'm older, thanks to you." His boots made a scuffled noise as he landed next to me.

"Margaret!" Seth yelled. "Let's go!"

"But-" Maggie said as she battled with Jay. "I'm...having...fun."

"Now!" Seth gritted his teeth.

"Fine!" Maggie said, angry. "We'll see you losers later." Maggie pushed Jay with all of her strength and bent down to the ground. She came up in a shower of sand and blinded Jay. Maggie laughed as she ran towards the hill that Brooke and I traversed. Seth and Lunk followed behind her protectively. I looked up at the hill and Brooke was nowhere to be seen.

"Stop them," Jay yelled to me.

"No, let them leave," said a voice behind Jay. I heard running footsteps get closer and closer until finally their owners appeared in my sight. The one in the lead had no feet; instead, he carried his body weight on two giant wings that sparkled in the light of the barrier. The other seven figures treaded behind in a uniform pattern behind Tensar. "We have a mission to do here," he said.

"Don't rush ahead of us like that, dude," Dane said as he slapped Jay on the back.

"If he didn't," I said getting up. "I'd be dead." I walked over to Tensar and the rest of them with my now swollen hands. All of them seemed prepared enough. Unlike Brooke and I, who didn't have any time to prepare for our vacation. Speaking of Brooke, where was she?

"Yeah, now I'm gonna kill you," Dane said, slapping me on the back. "Don't you ever scare anyone of us like that again. You could have been more rational when running after Brooke, even if she was mad. Speaking of her, I don't see her. Where's that brunette ran off to?"

"I don't know," I said, rubbing my back. "She just sorta disappeared when we were fighting The Shadow."

"She's fine," Jay said. "I saw her leave from the hill after I hit that big guy with some fireballs."

"Good," Tensar said. "But it would be best if she were here to run down the plan with Rick and the rest of you all."

"I'll recite it to her," I said. "What's up?"

"Hm, well, if you are positive," Tensar stopped floating and rested his legs on the beach. "The plan goes as this: Master and Headmaster have come to the conclusion that the Crystal is located in one of the Elemental Palaces. Deep in the bowels of one of them lies a stairway that leads to the Crystal of Life. But the trick is that all of the Palaces are made in mind only for Guardians whose element matches the Palace.

"It is said that any creature or any Guardian who enters a Palace that is not of their element shall be cursed forever and will have misfortune rained upon them all eternity by the fairies that enter their souls."

"But what about me?" I asked. "I technically am not associated with just one element."

"Exactly, Richard," Tensar said sadly. "The Masters and I have decided that it's best if you stay out of the Palaces and keep guard around the island."

"What?" I yelled. "Are you crazy? I wouldn't send any of those guys anywhere unless I was going with them. You can't just expect me to "keep guard" for who knows how long while my friends walk into million year old death traps!"

"I don't expect you to," Tensar agreed. "That is why I am staying with you. It's sort of like babysitting."

"I don't like this one bit," I said. "There has to be another way."

155

"This way is best," Tensar said. "I expect you to-" BOOM! The sea came crashing down on the shoreline.

I jumped into action and sprang toward the sound. There was a constant rumble underneath the ground that shook the entire beach. Something foreboding grew in my stomach and I decided to slow my road. Dane and the rest of them caught up with me when I stopped to take a breath.

"The ground is changing," Dane said. "It's not an earthquake..it's...something different."

"Well there's no use in just sitting here and thinking about it," I said. "Take us to where it's moving, Dane."

"Gotcha," he said as he took leadership. "This way…"

We treaded the beach and came up on some foothills. A giant figure loomed over top of one of the hills and that feeling in my stomach grew. Each step closer to the figure my heart rate increased. I swear my heart was beating out of my chest. But I was a Guardian. I wasn't scared of anything. At least I wasn't supposed to be. When we reached the top of the hill though, I didn't know what to expect. I know I didn't expect what I saw, though.

"Brooke?" I questioned. Yes, that was Brooke. But what I should have said was, "What the heck is that giant thing in front of you?!" Well, I could kinda guess what it was. That feeling in my stomach grew and I…I felt it inside of me. Luscious, precious water controlled the entire mighty world. It doused fire, weakened Earth, and chilled wind. I felt like I was no longer an Elemental Guardian…I was a Water Guardian.

"That must be the Water Palace," Keith said. "I *know* it's the Water Palace." We advanced on Brooke and the Water Palace with awe. It was gorgeous. Perfect exterior design that seemed to glow even in the darkness of Atlantis. There was no flaw that my eyes could see and I wondered how any human could or Guardian construct such a beautiful thing.

"I'm sorry I left," Brooke said. "It called to me."

"What the heck made the ground move like that?" Dane asked.

"The Palace was hidden when I got here," she explained. "When I called on it, though, it revealed itself."

"Seems like a defense mechanism," Tensar said. "I think we should expect the others to be the same. Brooke, let me explain to you to our plan to find the Crystal"

"Yeah," she said. "I already know, Master already explained to me. I'm ready to go in."

"I think we all are," Jay agreed.

"Let's get it!" Sam yelled to the Guardians.

The rest of them agreed and set out to their respected Palaces. Except me. I had a babysitter. Tensar reassured me that it would be "just like old times" and I just laughed and said that those days were over. But deep inside, sometimes I do wish I still was that kid who had no friends. That kid who loved Fiona but could do nothing about it. That kid who could see Fiona every day.

That kid who could see Fiona smile.

CHAPTER XVII

Signal

"This sucks," I said. Same probably went for the Imp Faerie that I was poking with a stick. Don't worry, they're considered vermin like rats or roaches. Eaugh, I hate roaches. I also hated sitting there in the Capitol gardens with Tensar the Pomega. Don't get me wrong, he's the Kool Kat of pomegas but I really wanted to be out kicking Maggie's butt.

"It is what you make it," Tensar said. "We haven't had a chance to catch up, don't you agree?"

"Yeah," I said. "Where have you been?" Ever since all of that Guardian crap happened, I had only talked to Tensar about three good times. I never saw him on Bikini Atoll. And of those three good times, meeting him here was one of them. I still remembered the first time I found out he could talk. That was after…you know what, never mind.

"Errands, my friend," he sighed. "I have been so busy keeping the creature world in order. I called for a Pomega gathering and found out that the others are not ecstatic about the whole Zane situation or The Shadow. They are even thinking about joining the battle. Pomega have not seen battle since the early days, before I was born. But enough about my affairs, how have you been?"

"I could write a book," I laughed. "But you'd have to experience it for yourself." I stood up from my spot on the ground. The little Imp scurried away to its hole hidden somewhere in the garden. Imps were probably the only vermin I was going to find in this trophy garden and the rest of the creatures were in the forest next to the Earth Palace. I hoped Dane and Sabrina were having a fun time.

"Tensar," I started. "I can't stay here. I have to fight. It's in my blood now. I always knew it was but something always held me back. When I found out that I was a warrior, that was the happiest day of my life. Now you're telling me that I can't do what I was born to do. I can't let you do that."

"Would you rather die?" Tensar asked. "That is the only other option. You're far more valuable to the Guardians alive than dead."

"Even great warriors die," I said. "Look at all of all of those bones on the beach. I wouldn't be the first to die and I certainly won't be the last. At least I would go out fighting."

"That is a Guardian's mentality," Tensar agreed. "But what you're talking about is suicide. That is not a Guardians path. It is almost as bad as evil. Evil corrupts." He nodded his head toward the glass statue of Vetro on top of the Capitol. "It leads to destruction. People die. Because they think they're better than everyone else. The

159

opposite also leads to evil, too. Zane was once a lonely child, as you know. He thought he was worthless, which led to his downfall. It's a sad fate but it is the truth."

"I won't end up like either of them," I smiled. "I promise." Now that he mentioned the statue, I became curious. I wasn't much of a history nerd but Guardian history was far more entertaining than human history. This was probably the only chance I would get to see the statue up close. And for some reason I had that strange foreboding feeling in my stomach again.

"Can we go see the Vetro statue?" I asked. There was something I had forgotten about dear old Vetro. "We already circled Atlantis twice and no sight of The Shadow."

"I think so," Tensar agreed. "You may ride on my back."

"No," I said. "I want to walk." And by walk, I meant run.

I ran through the green garden admiring the exotic flowers. How could they grow without sunlight? Maybe they were like moonflowers. But there was no moon there either. The enigma kept me occupied as I approached the Capitol. The giant building reminded me of a troll guarding a hidden secret in a fairy tale.

Once I approached the massive golden double doors of the Capitol, I paused to catch my breath. The feeling in my stomach was erupting now. I could feel it seeping into the rest of my body slowly with its flow. Everything seemed golden. I was living my life like it was golden. The golden doors were golden. Even the steel beside the doors. Of course, I had to touch it. I wiped away all of the old dust with my hand and revealed a symbol.

"Lightning?" I asked.

"I have no idea," Tensar admitted. "Maybe some tribute?"

"No," I said with confidence. "It's there on purpose. It's a signal."

Then I pushed open the double doors.

CHAPTER XVIII

I'm In The Middle of Some Calibrations

"Woah." Was all I could let escape my lips. Not just because of the golden interior or the magical ceiling that looked liked the morning sky. That woah was also partly because the lightning element dispersed from its cave inside my body. The other stuff was cool but it wasn't as amazing as that feeling I got.

"This is impressive," Tensar said as he floated inside with me. The entire main floor was dedicated to debating. In the middle of the room was a proud podium that stood on a platform with steps circling it. On both sides of the podium were two giant arched stairways that led to an upper balcony with wall-sized glass that showed the entire backside of the garden. It was so simple, yet so beautiful.

"The lightning element is strong here," I said walking up to the podium.

"Oh, no," Tensar gasped.

"What?" I asked.

"Then this must be the Lightning Palace," Tensar realized. "I should not be here. I am going to be cursed forever."

"No," I assured him. "The Lightning Palace is close. Very close. But this is not it. If it was, then every congressman that entered this building had to be an Elemental Guardian."

"You're right." Tensar joined me near the podium. "I should have felt the curse's effect by now."

"I feel powerful," I smiled. I grasped the sides of the podium and stood tall and proud. My Power Gloves were flowing with lightning. It felt good to let it out onto the podium. The electricity buzzed the entire room with its electric fury. It was as if the podium *needed* the lightning. It wanted more. More. MORE!

Lightning cackled outside behind me and I felt the power of the lightning. The roof of the Capitol began to open above me. The upper floors also moved in the same fashion, creating a way to the top. The podium began to rise Tensar and I slowly to the top of the Capitol. Each floor we passed had different designs from the bottom floor but still had the same golden color scheme.

The final room at the top of the Capitol was spherical in design with a dull gold finish. There was nothing there but a glass window that circled around the entire room. The glass made it possible to look at all of Atlantis at once. I was truly at the seat of power. Well, podium.

"This is cool," I said admiring the view. "Was this in anyone's history?"

"Not that I know of," Tensar admitted. "This room seems to be only available to users of the Lightning Element. Remember that people with your gift are very few." From the ceiling dropped a lightning rod that extruded just long enough for me to grab it. I had no idea what it would do but I knew how to work it. It was gonna do what lightning rods were meant to do.

"You might wanna leave the room." I told Tensar.

"Right," He said and jumped head first out of the window. The beautiful creature floated not too dangerously close to the window, watching. As if I had the world in my hand, I grasped the lightning rod with my right hand. Then, through all of my strength, I released the Lightning Element.

Electricity ran free in the room. Yes, I could feel it. I gripped the lightning rod and rose off the podium. Atlantis was mine. I could *feel* the entire Island. If I just closed my eyes, maybe I could see it, too. I felt the lightning rise through the top of the Capitol, no, it had transformed into the Lightning Palace. Through the roof and out through Vetro, the lightning traveled across Atlantis. It exposed all of the islands secrets to me.

I was Atlantis.

To the north, I traveled to the Wind Palace. The inside was pure white with barely any floors. Deep inside the tunnels of the Palace, I found Sam and Antoine. They were in there fighting these things. They were the same things we fought in the ruins of the Nightmare. Sam and Antoine were doing fine though. They seem to even be enjoying themselves.

To the west, I traveled to the Earth Palace. Everything was made of wood on the inside. I searched through the trees and found Dane and Sabrina fighting Lunk and Seth. While they were fighting, the hoards of zombies came pummeling after them, too. Lunk pretty much had the zombies covered while Seth fought the younger warriors. Dane and Sabrina were both tough cookies so I had no worries about them.

To the south, I traveled to the Water Palace. This Palace connected to the sea. It was as if the Palace was the sea. Through the vast darkness of the water, I found Brooke and Keith. They were underwater in a deep cavern. The entire cavern was inscribed with ancient text that I didn't have time to decipher. Brooke and Keith, however, seemed to be cracking the code.

To the east, I traveled to the Fire Palace. The Palace was full of fire. No, wait, it was *on* fire. Haphazardly, I searched around the Palace looking for Jay, Arlene and Lance. I searched and searched but I couldn't seem to locate any of them. No, I had to search harder. They had to be in there somewhere.

There, I saw Jay from a distance. His dark outline burst out of the flames holding something. As he ran closer to my vision I saw that he was holding, yeah, get this, Maggie. She laid in his arms, passed out and covered in soot all over her body. Jay's face was blank as he carried her to safety.

All of this happened simultaneously as I stood atop the Lightning Palace, taking the place of Vetro.

I hadn't searched one place, though. Down below the Palace there was something. Something ancient and strong. It couldn't have been the Nightmare. This ancient power was pure, clean. I could not see it, there was something blocking it. It didn't matter though, I knew where it was.

"Guys," I said to everyone. "I know where the Crystal is." The expression on everyone's faces changed to shock as I spoke in a whisper as the lightning carried my voice. I could control which general direction my voice went but not who heard it. I tried my best though.

"Where?" Keith asked. "We think we have the key to it. Brooke, am I the only one who hears Rick?"

"No," she said. "I hear him too. Where Rick? We have the code."

"What is it?" I asked them.

"Lightning," Keith sighed. "Took about two hours to get that answer."

"The Lightning Pal- I mean the Capitol. Meet me there," I said to everyone.

"Rick, I have a sort of problem," Jay sighed.

166

"I know," I said. "Bring her too."

I let go of the lightning rod and dropped back down to the podium. The lightning ceased and I felt powerless again. I signaled to Tensar that it was okay to come back inside and he rushed in. I patted him on his head and smiled.

"What happened?" He asked.

"I know where to find the Crystal of Life," I smiled. The podium slowly receded back to the bottom floor. I took the time to clear my head. Finally the moment I had been waiting for for weeks. All I had to do was get it, then I could bring Fiona back...

I jumped off the podium when it was a floor above the ground level. The pathway to the Crystal was somewhere in that room. I had a hunch, though. Old Vetro gave me an idea to what I had to do. Brooke and Keith's conclusion also proved my theory that I had to use the lighting element. That's why I ran up one of the giant staircases that led to the window in the back.

Lightning exploded from my hands, shocking each corner of the massive window. Then, slowly, I slashed an X over the entire frame. In my hands, I charged the electricity. It was forming. I had to make it huge. It grew, grew, grew until finally I let it loose into the middle of the glass.

The glare was spectacular. I covered my eyes because it was blinding me with the intensity of a thousand suns. After the glare simmered down, I looked over to see Tensar arriving. His eyes grew larger than normal when he saw what I had done. If pomegas could smile, he was doing it then.

Slowly, I turned around to the glass. Instead of glass, though, there was a tunnel. Not just any tunnel.

I had found the tunnel to the Crystal of Life.

CHAPTER XIX

Oh, You Again

"It's more caveman-ish than I expected," I said

"What, did you want a grand drape with flowers?" Tensar laughed.

"Rick!" Jay yelled from the doorway. Arlene straggled behind him looking pale as ever. Lance walked in with his usual swagger and air of arrogance. Maggie was still unconscious in Jay's hands as he ran up the steps to Tensar and I. Maggie had scorches all over her body and her armor was scarred. Jay laid her down next to Tensar as Arlene admired the passageway.

"What happened?" I asked as Tensar tended to Maggie.

169

"She tried to burn the place down," Arlene laughed. "But the place burned her. I don't know why Jay saved her. If it were up to me, I would have left her melt like the witch is."

"No one deserves to die like that," Jay spoke up. "Not even her."

As Tensar worked on his patient, Jay told me about his experience in the Fire Place. "It was crazy!" he recalled. Apparently, there were these fire things that protected about every level to the place and there were creatures he had never even heard of living in the gardens. Arlene didn't have as much of a fiery time as Jay did (she got her hair scorched when she almost fell in some lava). Everything was all fun and games until Ms. Maggie came and burned the place down. You would think that the Fire Palace would have precautions for that type of stuff. The Palace actually didn't burn down, though, the fire eventually went out.

Maggie's eyes finally opened after a few minutes. She blinked a couple of times and then she sat upright. She looked around and her eyes stopped on Jay. He stared back but stayed quiet. I would too if Maggie stared me down. Her lips parted and she spoke to Jay.

"You...saved me," she whispered.

"I'd do it again if I had to," Jay stared. "It's my job as a Guardian." I swear you could feel the awkward in the air. If you could measure awkward on some type of scale it would have been at about 100% right then. The look on Maggie's face was priceless. It was like confusion mixed with hate mixed with a little love. Just think about it, you just saved Satan, he wakes up, and you tell him that you would do it again. Yeah, just take a second to imagine that.

170

"Thanks, I guess," Maggie said as she stood up. Then she looked at the passageway. That's when things got worse. I honestly forgot about the giant magical passage that led to an even more powerful magical thing. "No way," she said as she gazed.

Clatter from outside announced that the rest of the crew had arrived. Dane came bursting into the door first trying to Earth Hammer down Lunk but to no avail. Antoine was Wind Striking him in the back, pushing the trio into the Capitol. Seth came crashing in with a wave of water. The remaining four Guardians filed in afterwards. The sight of all of those people made me laugh to myself.

"Seth! Lunk!" Maggie cried. She pointed to the passage. "The Crystal is this way!" And without a second thought, she ran.

I had no hesitation as I jump-started to chase behind her through the rocky passageway. Without turning around, I could hear the rest of them following us through the massive corridor. I tried to slow Maggie down by aiming attacks at her feet but she was swift and agile. She dodged them as if this was second grade math to her. I couldn't catch up with her, either. I just had to keep up.

After a few turns I had to stop. No, I wasn't tired. There just wasn't anywhere else to run. We had ran into the room we've all been waiting for. The Big Kahuna. And in the middle of that giant rock room, you may ask? Oh, it was gorgeous, all right. It was more gorgeous than any of the Palaces. I might even have to go this far: it was more gorgeous than Fiona. It was the mighty. The proud...

The Crystal of Life

Sorry for that overdramatic entrance. But, you know, you just have to imagine the feeling I got when I saw that thing. After all that build up, though, I never guessed that it would actually be something completely different. It laid there, in the palm of a giant statue of a man made of stone that I didn't recognize. Wait, no. I did recognize the man. It was the same statue outside of Baton Rouge's School for the Mind, Body, and Soul. Yeah, I have bad memory but I do remember that.

Back to what I was saying, though. The Crystal of Life wasn't actually a crystal.

It was a transparent vial.

Made of crystal.

The circular vial held some sort of magical liquid that emitted its own light that brightened the entire room with a blue hue. It was blinding, for sure. The light illuminated the entire statue all the way down to its boots. Surrounding the statue was a giant chasm that went further down than the light could reach. To get to the Crystal I would have had to leap across. I raised my arm to cover my eyes as the rest of the gang caught up and gazed at the Crystal. I didn't blame them. No one would have.

"Out of my way!" Maggie said as she pushed me aside. I was starting to like her style. Her style was perfect for Jay. They both were impatient. And the perfect example of that arose when Jay ran after her. I followed suit behind Jay but I was too slow. Maggie and Jay were halfway to the Crystal when Lunk caught up with me. I wasn't gonna catch up with them anyway so I turned around to face my enemy.

"Just give up," I said sternly. I didn't give him any time to respond. I immediately began to air palm him in his chest. His Earth Armor cracked as I hit it about five times at full force. He staggered backwards for a little bit and he caught his balance. That gave me time to look over to Maggie and Jay. They had made it to the statue and were dukeing it out. How ironic.

Lunk charged at me like I had a red drape in my hand. I braced myself with Earth Arms just in time as he collided with me. I'm pretty sure I slid a few feet when I tried to hold him off. I grabbed his shoulders and jumped behind him. With my back against his back, I tried out a new move. I had been practicing that move for about a month so I had my doubts about what the outcome would be.

To my surprise, it worked out perfectly. My elbow lightning shock hit him in the back and stunned him. Lunk fell to the ground as his feet gave from underneath him. I turned around and kicked him jokingly to make sure he wasn't gonna get up.

"Childs play, bro," I laughed. "You should go easy on the French fries next time. Your reaction time is a little slow." Speaking of food, I hadn't had a Meat Lovers' Pizza in like *forever*. This superhero stuff was cramping my stomach…literally.

Maggie showed no mercy to Jay as the fight raged on in the background. Metal against fire. Fire against metal. I watched in amazement like a little kid testing out his new hoverboard. My family was too poor to afford a hoverboard of our own so I just sat and watched the other kids glide around while I was at the park. Sigh, I was a lonely child. I blame it all on society. They shun the poor and –

Lunk grabbed my ankle. "By the way," he said. "I had a salad earlier." Earth slowly extruded from his hands and extended up my limb. Oh, I knew this little trick. Dane called it the Earth Coffin. It, well, you can basically guess what it does. I'm sure you're smart.

The sad thing about knowing about the Earth Coffin, though, was that Dane never told me how to get out of it. I couldn't just yell across the room to him and let him give me a crash course in avoiding coffins. I had to do like every other great superhero does...wing it.

I twisted my body and kicked Lunk in the face with my free leg. His arm sprung loose and I limped away. My lower right leg was completely encased in Earth and I dragged it along as I hopped away. "Stay back," I yelled as I threw fireballs at Big Boy. I swear he had this evil smile as he blocked my attacks with his Earth Arm.

Lunk stopped chasing me and raised his arms. With a massive force he dropped them down onto the cold floor. The ground cracked and rose up as the tremor advanced towards me. "Oh, crap," I said as I tried to jump in the air. My Earth cast was heavy as... well, Earth. The hungry attack spiraled toward me as I sat there like a sitting duck. Better yet, I was a deer mesmerized by incoming headlights.

Sabrina bounced in front of me and calmed the Earth with her hands. Without looking back, she grabbed my Earth leg and the Earth crumbled beneath her hand. "Go, I got 'em," she said as she sprinted toward Lunk. She sprinted forward, did a front flip, and tried to kick Lunk in the face. Lunk blocked her with an Earth arm and they engaged in battle.

Next objective: get to the Crystal. The rest of the Guardians were holding off Seth and some imitation Guardians. I looked around and I was the only one free. I had to do something. The entire world was counting on me. Like Atlas, the entire weight of the world was on my shoulders. The thought sent shudders through my body and I closed my eyes. After a moment I opened them and looked around. Then, I noticed Jay.

His movements were slow. Maggie was swift. Jay tried to Fire Palm Maggie but she quickly moved to the side. Usually, Jay would turn and continue to attack. I saw his hesitation, and he turned his head too slowly. Before he could look, Maggie was behind him with her sword, ready. Her lips parted into a evil smile and she prepped her sword. Unknowingly, Jay did a grave mistake of facing toward the front. "Bye, bye!" Maggie shouted as she pierced Jay's back with her sword.

"No!" I screamed.

Jay stared in horror at the bloody tip of the sword that extruded from his body. Slowly, Maggie slid the metal from Jay's body as if she was savoring the moment. Jay had no strength to keep his body stable so he collapsed to the ground without a sound. There was nothing I could do, I stood there in horror.

Maggie, on the other hand, leapt up and climbed the giant statue. Once she reached the hands, she grabbed for the Crystal. The light the Crystal illuminated was smothered by Maggie's hand as she took it from its resting place. She raised it up above her head as if she had just won the Superbowl. The light blasted from her hands as she jumped off of the statue.

The chasm was the only thing that separated Maggie and I. She sneered as she sprinted forward with the Crystal, eager to escape. Anger filled my blood as I ran to block her. She wasn't gonna get away if I had anything to do with it. She killed Jay. She…killed Jay. I was going to avenge him.

Maggie and I approached the chasm at blinding speed. A fight between us was inevitable. I braced myself and leapt into the air to face the leader of The Shadow. The one Jay saved. The one that killed Jay. Zane's daughter.

I saw it out of the corner of my eye. Fire. It came from the direction of the statue. As fast as it came it laced onto Maggie's ankles. Maggie cringed in fear as her skin burned. We were both in the air now. Maggie had her arms out. With the Crystal in them.

I grabbed the Crystal.

We both plummeted to the ground, both latched onto The Crystal of Life. It was either fall with the Crystal of let go and let Maggie have it. There was no way Maggie was getting that thing. I had to do what I had to do. I gripped the Crystal tight and fell towards the darkness of the chasm...

The tip of my toes touched the edge.

Maggie's toes touched the end of her side of the chasm.

Without each other, both of the Crystal and us would fall into the darkness of the deep hole. I looked over Maggie's shoulder and saw Jay slump quietly down as he leaned on the statue with a smile on his bloodied mouth. He was alive. All was well. Except that I was one step away from death. I think I've been in worse, though.

"Give me the Crystal," I begged Maggie. "We'll both be safe."

"Not over my dead body," she glared.

No one came to save us. We sat there for what felt like seven days and seven nights. My fingers loosely gripped the Crystal while I stared into the darkness below me. There was no way for me to get out of this without losing. All of that work and I just ended up like that. I had failed Master. I had failed my friends.

I had failed Fiona.

"Enough," Seth said from behind me. "I think it's time to bring in our ace in the hole."

Maggie smiled uncontrollably. "Perfect."

"Bring them in," Seth yelled to someone. I stared at Seth's reflection in the Crystal while I held it. I had a clear view of what was behind me. Two imitation Guardians walked in from the entrance. Each had dragged in two large boxes. Human sized boxes. The sound of the fake Guardians sliding the boxes across the rocky floor was eerie enough to make the rest of the Guardians watch in amazement. The fake Guardians hauled the boxes to Seth who stood right in the vision of the Crystal.

"Richard Raines. Rick as they call you," Seth started. "Today, right now, you shall have a judgment of character. Before you, I have two coffins. The first one," he grabbed the one nearest to him. Seth grabbed the top ledge and pulled. The lid fell to the ground with a sickening boom. "contains my dear father, Zane."

I glared into the Crystal. There he was, in the coffin, dead. His body was not decayed. I remembered earlier when I saw the ancient bones of past Guardians. There was no doubt that Guardian bodies lasted a long time.

"If you give up the Crystal," Seth continued. "We will revive our father."

"Why would I do that?" I said impatiently. "You're crazy."

"Some might say that," he said in a dull voice. "You asked why you would help revive our father. This is the reason why." Seth grabbed the top lid of the other coffin. His fingers pried open the wood slowly and it popped apart with a *snap*. Seth slowly let the lid fall to the ground with a huge echo that vibrated around the room. I stared hard into the Crystal to see the other body. I recognized the body. "No…" I whimpered.

CHAPTER XX

Consequences

Fiona had her eyes closed as if she were sleeping. I wish she was sleeping. Deep inside, though, I knew she was dead. A rush of emotions slammed into my head as I stared at her lifeless body. All of the sadness. All of the anger.

It would have all ended if I just dropped into the darkness. Then, I would be with her for sure. That was the only way out of that nightmare. The Nightmare may be the physical embodiment of terror but that, that was real terror. I kept thinking to myself, "If I just dropped down it would all be over…" But is that really what Fiona would have wanted?

"If you give us the Crystal and let us revive our father this will all be over," Seth said. "If not, Fiona goes into the chasm."

Fiona was already dead, so did it matter? Yes, it did. It was the principle of it. But then again, did I really want Zane to be alive again? Did I really want that man to see daylight again? Did I really want to for just a dead body?

But it wasn't just any dead body.

I felt as if there was still a tiny piece of her still left in her flesh. There had to be. What else would preserve a body in perfect condition for a year? Would I really give up possibly the world for a chance that there was still part of her on this Earth somehow? That was the real question. I knew the right answer, the moral answer, but yet it somehow felt wrong.

"Rick," Fiona called inside of my head. I hadn't heard her voice in forever. The echoes she gave me ceased and I thought she would never disturb me again. But at the final moment, judgment day, she called me again. I did not answer.

"Drop the Crystal," she begged. "I'll be fine. I promise. Your job is to protect the world, not babysit me, Rick. Go save Jay instead. I-"

"No, Fiona," I said aloud. A rush of sad emotions from an outside force swam through my brain. Was that Fiona? No matter, I had made my mind up. I thought I had came to the right choice.

"Seth, you play a sick game," I started. "Only purely evil people like you would come up with something like this."

"I take that as a compliment," he chuckled.

"I know the right decision, though," I sighed. I slid my hands to the bottom of the Crystal. If I had stayed like that for more than a second I would have fell into the chasm. In less than a second

181

though, I pushed myself, Maggie and the Crystal into the air. Maggie still held onto the Crystal as she leaned upwards out of the chasm. Once we were both fully standing I sighed in desperation.

"Go ahead," I waved to Maggie. "Do what you have to do."

"No!" Sabrina yelled. Lunk pinned her down but she was still kicking.

"Shutup," he simply said.

Maggie leapt across the crevice and walked right past me without glancing. Her boots echoed across the stone floor as she made her way to her brother. The liquid in the Crystal shone brightly across the room, making it as if she carried a light in her hands. The sound of boots hitting stone stopped when Maggie had reached her destination. Without hesitation, she handed the Crystal of Life to Seth.

"It should only take one drop," he said. He poked the Crystal with his right index finger. From the tip of his index spiraled a small amount of Earth that drilled into the case of the Crystal. Once the Earth was about half an inch in it, flattened on the inside surface of the Crystal. He gripped the case with his other hand and he pulled with his free one.

The glass cracked a little on the sides where he pulled. Eventually, though, he had managed to create a small hole in the Crystal. It sort of reminded me of a ritual. Seth stepped towards Zane and placed the Crystal up to his lips.

"Drink, father," Seth said as he slowly tilted the Crystal to Zane's mouth. Everyone stared in awe as a drop of the liquid separated itself from its friends. Seth tilted the vial more. The drop was at the hole. Seth tilted some more.

The Liquid of Life fell into Zane's mouth.

It wasn't instant. It wasn't even magical. It was like he was awakening from an ancient slumber. First, his eyes gingerly parted. Then he blinked. Then he blinked again. He did an intake of fresh air from his nose and let it out through his mouth. Next came the limbs. He creepily stretched out his muscles, careful not to hurt anything. For a long time he stared at his son. Then he spoke.

"Seth?" Zane asked in a weak voice.

"Father?" Seth stared in amazement.

Maggie and Lunk both yelled "Father!" at the same time and rushed to Zane and Seth.

"No, stay back," Seth warned. "We don't know what might happen."

Zane licked the inside of his mouth as if it were dry. "I believe...I had died. Am I right, son?"

"Yes," Seth agreed. "About a year ago."

"Ah," Zane spoke. "So my children have taken my advice to fine the Crystal of Life?"

"Yes, father," Maggie said obediently.

"I hear Margaret is well. Who else is here?" Zane questioned.

"Lunk," Seth sighed.

"...and?" Zane asked.

"Rick and his posse," Seth looked down.

183

"Never mind them," Zane coughed. "Where's Elisa?"

Dead silence.

"I see," Zane ended the silence.

"Why didn't you tell us about the Nightmare?" Maggie asked as she stepped up to her father. "How come I'm not Disturbed?"

"That old thing…" Zane pondered. "The Nightmare is my pet, simply put. I can feel its presence in this place. I assume, though, that this is not its resting place. It came here for a reason. I shall deal with it later. As for your sister, well, she was an experiment. I wanted to see how much of the Nightmare's power could a human being take. Elisa had it, alright. But you both were so young. Your sister, she didn't know what she was doing. One day she just simply *wooshed* some of her powers into the wind and like a little insect, you caught some of it. Don't ask me how that worked, I just witnessed it. It's a pity that she's gone, I would have liked to tell her. I'm pretty sure, though, that she had it figured out."

His laugh echoed throughout the entire room.

"Still your old self, I see." I spoke up.

"Rick, my dear boy!" Zane said excitedly. "I didn't know you were here. Excuse me, I am not myself right now. There are a lot of effects to the Crystal of Life, it seems."

"I just want the Crystal," I said.

"Ooh," He sighed. "That old thing? Seth, bring it to me." Seth raised the Crystal to his father. Zane reached out his trembling hands to receive his gift. Seth was reluctant to give away his prized possession but he had to obey his father. Zane latched onto the Crystal and Seth backed away, as if the Crystal were now acid.

184

"Rick...come here," Zane said in a lazy voice. There was still a chance that I was going to get the Crystal and revive Fiona. This would have been an easy win. There had to still be some heart left in Zane. I knew there had to be. It was my last hope...

Or I could just snatch it from him.

I approached his phantom coffin with caution. Seth and Maggie let me by and I stood only a foot away from Zane. He looked fragile. His body was still shaking. His skin showed a little age but nothing severe. He licked his lips with his dry tongue. It retracted back into his mouth like a dead snake.

"Why do you want this, Rick? Why do you oppose me?" He asked.

"I want it..." I paused. "I want it to bring Fiona back to life."

"The one that I killed?"

"Yes."

"I see." Zane looked me directly in the eye. I stared deep into his soul and there was nothing; emptiness. The dead snake came out of his mouth and he licked his lips again. "Let this be a lesson to you, Rick; no one messes with Zane."

Then he dropped The Crystal of Life.

There was no time to react.

I couldn't move.

It took a trip to the stone floor.

And it shattered into a million pieces beneath my feet.

185

CHAPTER XXI

The Meaning of Love

A drop of The Liquid of Life splashed onto my face. The rest, gone. My heart, gone.

Fiona, gone.

I felt like the entire world just shattered right before my eyes. It felt worse that when Fiona died. This time I had a chance to save her. I had a chance.

I had a chance.

"Why…" I sobbed. It wasn't a question. I got down on my knees and grabbed at the shards of glass. I crushed them in my hands, not worrying about the bleeding. I wanted to bleed. I wanted to die. There was nothing else left worth fighting for.

Not Jay.

Not Brooke.

Not the Gang.

Not Master or Headmaster.

Not the world.

Just Fiona.

She was the reason I stepped up to be leader. She was my first love. My first girlfriend. My first kiss. My first everything…

And then there was no way to bring her back. So there was no way to bring my happiness back. When she died, I went into shock. I didn't talk to anyone for weeks. I suppressed my emotions by fighting, training. That's what she would have wanted, right? When I heard that there might have been a way to bring her back my hope had been restored. I had a purpose for all of that training. There was reason behind it.

But then, it all shattered right beneath my feet. My entire life. The reason I did the things I did. I did them for her. And to see all of my hard work shattered on the ground…there was no coming back from that.

I wanted the pain to be there. I wanted it to take over my senses. I know I was screaming but it was my body reacting. My mind was somewhere else. In a stupor. A trance. Where was her voice now? Gone. Just like my hopes.

Not even her spirit was with me anymore.

"We have no more business here," Zane said in another world. "Carry me away my children."

"Stop them," someone said.

"No, let them leave." Said another. I think Tensar had joined us.

"Wise choice," Zane replied. "We will meet again, young warrior "

That's all I heard. I wasn't concerned. I didn't care. Honestly, I didn't care.

It was just me, Tensar and nine other people.

And Fiona.

Without thinking, I leapt on Fiona's dead body. Someone called my name, I think it was Jay, but I ignored him. The coffin dropped to the ground with Fiona and I in it. The glass had fallen from my hands and I was gripping the sides of Fiona's arms.

Bitter tears fell from my eyes but more rapidly.

They dripped onto her gorgeous face.

I leaned in closer to get a better look. One last look. Her face was as flawless as ever. Around her neck though, were marks from where she was Force Chocked by Zane. Somehow, the marks on her skin weren't an imperfections. It was part of her complexion. I found that my hand had moved on its own toward her neck.

If I closed my eyes I could not tell that the scar was there. A wise man once told me, "Blind people have such pretty eyes because they haven't seen the ugly of the world. They may hear it, but their eyes cannot be exposed and that's a blessing." He was right. I could not see the evil of Zane's ways; I could only feel the soft skin of Fiona.

When I opened my eyes back up a couple of tears slid down my cheek. I felt them run down my face.

Down, down, down.

Then they stopped for a second because they hit another wet spot on my cheek.

Then they continued their journey down.

Down.

Then they fell into Fiona's mouth.

"It only takes one drop," Seth had said earlier.

I had three.

I didn't know it but I had three.

I had never believed in miracles until that moment. Up until then, I always thought everything bad that could possibly happen happened to me.

First, her eyes parted. Then, she blinked. Then she blinked again.

I felt her breathe in.

"Fuh...," I was lost. "Fiona?"

She took in another breath. Then her breath escaped her mouth and hit my face. "...Rick?"

No, it couldn't have been true. It was too good to be true. "Fiona," I sobbed.

Slowly, she raised her arms around me. Then she grabbed my back. "Rick," was all she said. That's all she had to say. I eased my way onto her body then I slid my face on the side of hers.

Tears poured down my face. Not tears of sorrow, tears of happiness. "You came back for me," she whispered in my ear. I could hear her start to cry. "That's the most anyone has ever done for me."

I heard footsteps surround the coffin. I didn't care, they could watch. I embraced Fiona as we both cried our eyes out. She held me closely and slowly caressed my back. I knew everyone was still watching. I could feel them. They didn't matter anymore.

I had Fiona.

And that's all that mattered.

CHAPTER XXII

The Other Rick

Saturday, August 11th, 2068. The afternoon sun blazed in the top portion of my vision. I was just lying on the beach. You know, thinking about a lot stuff. No one really takes time out to just sit down to think to themselves anymore. Trust me, everyone should do it every once and a while. It helps you think over your problems and goals in life. Currently, though, I didn't think I had any problems. I deserved time to relax. I also deserved a gold medal, pizza, ice cream and a hoverboard.

But anyways, I was still exhausted from Atlantis. I needed a break from this superhero stuff. After a while it gets old. And I know you're thinking, "Rick, you can fly and shoot water out of your hands. How could that possibly get old?" Well, let me tell you. I was still just a kid. A kid who hadn't even finished high school. A lonely kid at that.

Imagine in a day everything you knew completely changed. One moment you were nobody then the next, you're the most important person in the world. I never had time to reflect back on that. If I did, I'd probably be dead by now. But now that there is time to reflect, I honestly don't know how I got through it. I think I really had to be a superhero to do that.

A figure appeared before the sun and blocked out some of the light overhead. I groaned. I never got a break, did I?

"If Antoine got his head stuck in the microwave again then I'm not moving," I said, agitated.

"Actually, It's not that this time," Lance said.

"Then what is it? You know this is my off time."

"Rick wants to see you," Lance said blankly.

"The driver?" I was interested. I clutched the sand with my hands and lifted myself up. I dusted off my clothes and grabbed my sword off the ground. "Where is he?"

"At the infirmary," Lance had little emotion. "He checked in while we were in Atlantis."

"Thanks, Lance." And I was on my way. Rick the Driver, hunh? I remembered the first time I had met him. He was the guy that brought me to B.R.S.M.B.S. Since then, though, he seemed to stay away from the all of the action. I didn't even know what type of Guardian he was. And we never really talked. Why did he want me? Why not Master or Headmaster or any of the other Guardians? Well. It seemed like everyone needed me.

I walked down the main path of Bikini Atoll waving to all of the girls. I even saw Kristyn, the Bully. As I walked by her she gave me a snarl and bumped into my shoulder. I guess she still didn't like me for not bowing down to her in the cafeteria. I was better than that. And she was probably still angry at the fact that she couldn't do anything about it. I hadn't heard about her bullying anyone ever since that last fight we had on the stage.

That's all Zane was, too, a big bully. A tougher one, true, but he could be stopped. I stopped him before, right? So it couldn't be hard a second time. That's what I told myself, anyway. Zane was in a different league than Kristyn.

"Wassup. Bro?" I said to Dane as we walked up to each other. He was in his regular clothes like the rest of my Squad and Squad B.

"Nothin', man," He laughed. "How's Jay and Fiona?"

"Jay's still a little hot-headed because obviously he can't be hurt. In his defense, though, this is the second time he's been bedridden in two weeks," I said. "And Fiona's been very quiet. The Crystal's powers seem to come slowly because she still feels weak. Either that or being dead has its toll on the body."

"Just let them both rest," Dane put his hand on my shoulder. "I'm sure they'll be fine. Sabrina and Antoine are bedridden, too. They'll be alright. You should go check on

Brooke, though, man. She hasn't been right since we got back."

"Where is she?" I asked.

"Over there," Dane said as he pointed to the makeshift park nearby. Oh, great. It was right through the path I had to take.

"I'll go by there," I said.

"Alright, bro. I'll catch you later." He said as he started to walk off. "And take a break, too, you look like you saw a nightmare." He laughed.

Funny, funny, I thought to myself. I had seen a few nightmares physically and mentally. My newest nightmare was talking to Brooke. I mean there she was right in my vision and then *BAM*, Fiona jumps in and takes over. It wasn't my fault. I tried to push Brooke away and now she has to face the consequences of her actions. That's like someone telling me not to touch fire and I touch it and get burned anyway. Even Fire Guardians aren't immune to being burnt.

Unlike most people, I was ready to face my nightmare. Whatever happened with Brooke was gonna happen. I wouldn't have avoided it for long anyway. Might as well have just gotten it out of the way then. No harm done, right? Right?

"All guys are the same," Sam said to Brooke. Oh, boy. They were having girl talk. Brooke and Sam were perched on a bench talking to each other. Sam had a stern look on her face while Brooke had a sadder expression.

"But what about Dane?" Brooke asked.

"He's a special case," Sam explained. "Look, I've known Rick longer than you have. There was nothing in the world that he wanted more than Fiona. Seeing her alive is like a fairy tale come true for him. You gotta put yourself in his shoes."

"I just wanna know what Fiona did to get him like that. I wish he would like me like that," Brooke said.

I had had enough of their girl talk. I also didn't want to hear anything I didn't want to so I showed myself while I was ahead. Both of the girls shushed when I walked into their view. Sam patted Brooke on the back, got up, and walked away. She gave me one of those death glares as she passed by me. I sighed a little bit as I walked up to Brooke.

I sat next to her and said nothing. There was nothing to be said. I'm a boy, though, what do I know?

"You're just like the boys back home," Brooke said.

"How's that?" I asked.

"So nice and down to Earth when you first meet them but when you let them into your heart they crush it from the inside," She sneered.

"I felt that I had given you enough warning, Brooke," I sighed.

"I know, but you still pulled me closer," she said. "Closer into what, Rick? Sadness, that's what."

"I didn't pull you closer, Brooke," I argued.

195

"You did!" she cried. "You just did, okay?" She stood and covered her face. I knew she was crying. She just didn't want me to see her tears.

"Look," I stood up behind her. "I'm sorry, I really am. Maybe when Jay gets better-"

She turned around. "Don't you dare put me on Jay," Her face was suddenly in a fit of rage. "You are a jerk."

And she slapped me.

"I deserved that," I lied.

"Yeah, you did!" she yelled. "Don't you ever treat another girl like you treated me," she hissed. She poked her pointer finger deep into my chest and made me fumble on my feet. She made an unpleasant gesture with her hand and stormed away.

Well, that could have gone far worse.

Way worse.

I slowly opened the door to Rick's hospital room. It was all white. There was nothing in the room except a white rectangle that extended from the wall. On the rectangle laid the other Rick. He had his eyes closed so I advanced with noise.

"Rick, you're finally here," He said. "At the rate you were coming, I would have been gone before you got here."

"Are you dying?" I asked.

"Sort of," He ushered me over. "Come here."

I approached with caution. If he had a contagious disease I didn't want to catch it. He reached down and grabbed the bottom of his shirt. And when he pulled it up I really couldn't say anything about it.

"Oh," I said, disgusted. "I don't think I can help you with that."

There was literally a giant gaping hole in the middle of his chest, slowly expanding.

"You caused it," he said. "The future is changing."

"Does it hurt?" I asked. I was a little more concerned for his health right then.

"It causes so much pain that I can't even comprehend it," Rick started. "But to answer your question, yes it does."

"How did I cause it?" I was curious.

"Somehow you changed the future," He said. "The future that I come from no longer exists."

"You're from the…future?" I asked. It wasn't really that surprising. We hadn't created time travel yet but in the past year had seen so much crazy stuff that I could believe time travel was possible. I mean, I didn't believe people could control the elements.

"The near future," He said. "A future where Zane ruled the entire world. He came into power and every country bowed down to him." His legs and arms started disappearing.

"The Guardians couldn't stop him?" I asked. He was starting to disappear more quickly.

"No one could as long as I was on his side," he said. I was about to become angry at him. "Shh, quiet. Let me speak, we don't have much time. I realized I was wrong for helping him so I found a way back. I had to change my decision somehow. The technology to bring me back had a few kinks in it so it brought me back a little too far. For about a year, I waited until it was time for you to meet Headmaster Ravenhawl. I made sure you got there safely and that's it. If I were to interfere with you directly, I would have made the future more corrupt than it already was. So, I stayed in the background, changing things.

"Not many things I tried changed your actions. I don't even know how the future changed. But something you did in Atlantis changed the future. Don't even ponder on what you did. It is done now."

His entire lower half was gone now.

"So, you sacrificed yourself for me to have a better life?" I asked in amazement.

"I sacrificed myself for the entire universe," He corrected. "That's what Guardians do, right?" He laughed and suddenly his laugh turned into a cough.

"Wow," I said. "That's so noble of you. I promise your sacrifice won't be in vain. I'll do everything I can to stop Zane."

"His time will come like mine is about to come now," He said. Rick was nothing left but just a head. "You would recognize who I am if I could remove my skin mask but as you can see, I have no hands," he laughed.

"Tell me who you are so I can give you honor," I begged.

"Eh, I'll tell you later," He laughed. "Just remember one thing before I go."

"What?" I asked. "What is it?"

"It's up to you to choose between Brooke and Fiona," He smiled. "They both become great people." He was a pair of floating eyes and lips.

"Wait," I asked quickly. "How do you know all of this?"

Even though I already knew the answer.

His whisper of a voice came from the empty bed.

"Because we are both Rick,"

"Rick Raines."

EPILOGUE

Beignets, Brawn, and Beauty

August 25, 2068.

"Are you sure you don't want any more hot chocolate?" she asked.

"No, I'm fine," I protested. "You guys enjoy yourselves."

"Suit yourself," Fiona laughed as she grabbed my mug. She had recovered mostly since Atlantis and I decided to take her and Jay out to Uncle Ed's. It had been a while since all three of us had been together and what would be a better place than Uncle Ed's?

I laughed as Fiona gulped down a whole plate of beignet fingers and got sugar all over her mouth. Jay just sat there picking at his food. He really wasn't much of an eater. Maggie's sword had barely missed his spine and ripped his stomach almost in half. He couldn't eat too much of anything for a while.

"It would be nice, Fiona, if I didn't get powdered sugar all over my nice shirt." Jay sneered.

"Loser," she said as she gulfed down more beignets.

"She can eat, can't she?" Uncle Eddy said as he walked up to our table.

"Like a vacuum cleaner," Jay remarked.

"You might wanna watch yourself, missy, or you might get a gut like mine!" Eddy laughed. "I'm just messin' with you."

Eddy slapped her too hard on the back.

Fiona coughed up the food she was eating and everyone burst out into laugher.

"Not funny," she said.

"I think it is," Jay responded.

"I gotta agree with Jay," I laughed.

"What?" she exclaimed. "Ugh, I hate you guys."

"You know you love us," I said. "How could you not?"

"Many ways, Rick" she said. "Don't get me started."

"Please don't," Jay said as he sipped his milkshake. "Or I might have to find a new set of ears."

"You know what, I actually kinda want a milkshake now," I said. "Can I have some, Fiona?"

"Go get your own," she retracted her frosty drink from me.

"I'll go get one for you," Uncle Eddy said. "Chocolate?"

"Of course," I said.

"I'll be right back," Eddy said. He started to walk towards the back. Then when he was halfway there he stopped as if he just realized something. Then he came back towards us.

"Wassup, Unc?" I questioned.

"I almost forgot," he said. "I think y'all would love to know that the old school should be back up and running in about a year or two. Y'all can finally get off that island and come home."

"Sweet. Will you be teaching there?" I asked.

"You know I'm retired, Rick," He said. "But I might stop by every once in a while."

"Don't we already have enough crazy teachers?" Jay asked.

"Don't you ever shut up?" Fiona giggled.

"Don't you ever stop being annoying?" Jay asked.

202

"You both are quite annoying, actually," I said.

"Hey!" Fiona said. "You're not a walk in the park either, mister."

"Yeah," Jay agreed. "Just wait until you see how grumpy he is in the morning."

"I'd be grumpy too if I had to see your face every day," Fiona replied.

"Burn," I said.

Jay sighed. "When will she stop picking on me?" He asked.

I laughed, "It's just the beginning."